Death's
Silent
Judgement

D1472013

Death's Silent Judgement

Anne Coates

URBANE
Publications

urbanepublications.com

First published in Great Britain in 2017
by Urbane Publications Ltd
Suite 3, Brown Europe House, 33/34 Gleaming Wood Drive,
Chatham, Kent ME5 8RZ
Copyright © Anne Coates, 2017

A CIP catalogue record for this book is available
from the British Library.

ISBN 978-1-911331-35-3
EPUB 978-1-911331-36-0
MOBI 978-1-911331-37-7

Design and Typeset by Michelle Morgan

Cover by Julie Martin

Printed and bound by CPI Group (UK) Ltd, Croydon, CR0 4YY

urbanepublications.com

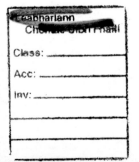

For my darling Harriet

I yet my silent Judgment keep,
Disputing not what they believe:
But sure as oft as Women weep,
It is to be suppos'd they grieve.

Mourning by Andrew Marvell

ONE

January 1994

The first thing that hit her was the smell and it made her gag. A mixture of odours, chemical and the metallic tang of blood, combined in an unholy alliance. An alliance which threatened to make the contents of her stomach evacuate in protest. She held a handkerchief to her face and tried to control her breathing – and the desperate urge to run out of the room. As her eyes became accustomed to the gloom, her glance took in the chaos, the overturned chair, the broken glass, the contents of Liz's briefcase scattered across the floor and then her brain registered what her heart had cried out against – Liz's inert body draped across the make-shift dentist's chair.

She made herself walk the four paces which brought her to the body and the certain knowledge that Liz Rayman was dead.

"Right, let's go through it one more time. You arrived here at 6.50pm. There was no one around when you entered the church and you saw no one as you made your way downstairs to the room she was using?"

"No." Hannah Weybridge sipped the cup of water that had just been handed to her by a young constable. "I mean yes, that's right." She could still taste the bile she had brought up, vomiting by the steps outside, just after she had phoned the police. Thank heavens for mobiles, she wouldn't have trusted her legs to carry her to a phone box. She shuddered. What was the point of all this repeated questioning? It must be obvious – even to the police sergeant sitting at the other side of the table in the vestry – that she wasn't the murderer.

"How long had you known Miss Rayman?"

Had. Hannah hated the man for his use of the past tense. What an insensitive pig. "About ten years," she replied quietly. Forever, said her heart. Liz had been a real soul mate. They had met at a New Year's Eve party given by a mutual friend who had a small flat in Fulham. Everyone had seemed to know everyone else – except Hannah and Liz who had gravitated towards each other. They had both come to the party alone but neither showed any interest in the spare males who hovered nearby then decided to try their luck elsewhere. That night they'd talked about books and books led them to the theatre that turned out to be a passion with them both. They toasted the New Year in champagne and parted in the early hours.

Liz had rung a few days later with an invitation to see the new Ackbourn play. Their friendship had flourished ever since through their various relationships with men and Liz's decision to take a sabbatical from her dentistry practice and join a medical charity in Africa. A choice Hannah had found both unfathomable and hurtful. She had been away for the birth of Hannah's daughter whom she'd named after Liz.

"Ten years," she repeated in a whisper. She shuddered. The cold had penetrated her heavy coat and scarf. Bone-chilling. The shock of what she had seen was mind-numbing. Her hand began shaking so much that the water spilled from the paper cup she was holding. She put it down on the table in front of her.

"And what were you doing here this evening?" The sergeant's eyes, with crow's-feet at the outer corners suggesting a happier side to him, were bloodshot from tiredness or perhaps ill health. His mousey hair had outgrown its cut and curled slightly over his collar. But there was nothing mousey about the way he looked at her. More rat-like.

Hannah wanted to scream. She'd already told them what she was doing there: she had arranged to meet Liz at the "mission" as she called it, before going to dinner. "She had something important to tell me," and she didn't want to say it in the the nearby Italian restaurant where the tables were set so close together you could almost hear the other diners breathing let alone confiding secrets. Hannah had been intrigued both to hear Liz's news and to see where her friend worked one day a week, giving free dental treatment and advice to the down and outs who inhabited the environs of Waterloo. The Bull Ring. Cardboard City.

Hannah, who knew the area well from her IPC Magazines days, had walked past St John's countless times but had never been inside the church. To her it's Grecian pillars were nothing more than a landmark on the south side of Waterloo Bridge. She was curious that Liz should be practising there. Apparently the priest ran a soup kitchen and, when he'd met Liz at some fund-raising function linked to the charity work she'd been doing in Somalia, had prevailed upon her good nature and inveigled her into opening a walk-in clinic.

Some clinic, thought Hannah. Liz had to carry all her instruments and supplies with her and had to do all her sterilising back at her Barbican practice. As she never had a dental nurse with her, she used to dictate notes about the patient's dental condition into a small dictaphone.

"The dictaphone!"

"I'm sorry Miss?"

"Look for her dictaphone! Liz always used it to dictate her notes maybe it'll hold some clue, maybe the murderer's voice..." Hannah had half risen from her chair but seeing the sergeant's patronising smile that was really more of a grimace, she sank back down and rested her head in her hands. Any minute now she would wake up and this awful interview would would fade from her consciousness.

Hannah closed her eyes and then opened them quickly to chase away the image of her friend's lifeless body, her throat slashed, her eyes staring out of a face which looked remarkably composed for someone who had just been brutally murdered. It suddenly occurred to Hannah that if she had arrived any earlier she might have been a witness – a dead witness an inner voice corrected. For why should whoever killed Liz leave Hannah alive to tell the tale?

"I'm sorry," said Hannah as she just managed to turn away in time to throw up into a waste paper basket.

"I'll get a car to take you home."

Ashen faced, Hannah nodded her thanks. Within minutes she was being ushered through the crypt corridors by a young policewoman. As they passed the room that had been Liz's surgery, Hannah took in the blaze of lights and a photographer shooting the dead body from every conceivable angle. Hannah shuddered. There's no dignity and certainly no privacy in death, she thought. At least not in a violent one.

The icy night air was like a slap in the face. A small crowd had gathered by the steps leading up to the church behind the police tape. Two policemen opened up a passage for Hannah and her companion to pass through. Hannah was aware of a murmur then a shout.

"Hey, Lady, what the hell's going on in there?"

Hannah glanced in the the direction the voice had come from and her eyes were held by an imposing figure that seemed to stand a head above the crowd. His mane of white hair was brushed away from his lined and craggy face and he stood proud despite the fact that his clothes were rags and he carried his home in a battered suitcase.

Hannah shook her head, grateful for the steadying arm of the policewoman. As the car set off she looked back to see that the man seemed to be staring after her. Perhaps he was one of Liz's patients. Silently the tears rolled down her face and she tried to brush them away with the back of her hand. The policewoman handed her an extra-strong mint.

"I always carry them with me now." She smiled and Hannah noticed the shadows beneath her eyes. "I don't think I'll ever get used to it."

"I hope you don't," said Hannah, wishing she could rid herself of the sickening image of her friend's dead body and of the question resounding in her head. Why Liz? Why?

TWO

"Hi. How are you?" Tom Jordan's voice was warm and familiar.

Hannah's throat tightened; tears were threatening to choke her and she struggled to keep her voice normal. If only Tom were with her now. What she really needed and wanted above all else was to feel his arms around her. To have him by and on her side. That was the dream. She was in the nightmare. "I'm fine, I... you sound as though you're in the next room."

"I wish I was." Tom chuckled. The sound of his laughter was her undoing.

"So do I... Oh Tom..." Hannah swallowed several times, fighting to control the emotion that was threatening to overwhelm her again.

"What is it Hannah? Nothing's happened to Elizabeth, has it?" The alarm in his voice was palpable.

"No Elizabeth's fine. It's Liz, my friend Liz Rayman. She's dead."

"Oh Hannah, I'm so sorry. I..." His breathing was regular again. The thought that someone might still be able to get to Hannah was never far from his mind. Her involvement with a prostitute had led to their meeting while he had been seconded to the BT police at Kings Cross. There were still so many unanswered questions surrounding the murders. Gerry Lacon had been deported back to South Africa but there were always influential people around who had had connections with the racket Lacon had been running. And Hannah was so vulnerable... For that reason he had been reluctant to accept the exchange posting to New York. But in some ways he thought he could be a better protection for her if he played the game and kept on the right side of the powers that be.

"She was murdered, Tom, and I... and I..." Hannah sniffed noisily. "I found her, Tom," she said quietly.

"Shit! When did this happen?"

"This evening." Hannah's voice was small. She sounded like a frightened child.

"Is anyone with you?"

"No. James is on his way. Lucky he was at home really – a minor miracle given the hours he puts in at that hospital. The policewoman who brought me home stayed for a while." Hannah wasn't sure if it was just the time lag on the transatlantic call or was the pause a bit longer at her mention of James? Janet, Elizabeth's nanny, had offered to stay on but Hannah wanted the comfort of a friend, not an employee.

"Which nick is investigating?"

"I don't know. It happened at St John's in Waterloo. Oh there's the bell – it must be James."

"Right. I'll find out what I can and ring you back." Tom's tone was brusque, business-like.

Hannah stifled a sigh. "Thanks. Bye." What she had wanted to hear was that he'd get the next flight back. Evidently that was not to be.

James took one look at her, wrapped his arms around her and hugged her tightly. She felt herself relax against him and smelt the cold night air on his navy duffle coat as her tears flowed. Gently he unwound his arms.

"Let me get this coat off." He shrugged the coat to the floor then with his arm around her shoulders led her into the sitting room. Alongside her on the sofa, he took her hands in his, his deep brown eyes full of concern. "Tell me."

Hannah told him about her discovery of Liz's body and the police questioning. She closed her eyes then opened them quickly. "I don't think I'll ever get that sight and ghastly smell out of my mind, James. It was – horrible seems too mild a word. Nothing can describe …"

"Don't try." He pulled her towards him and held her close. Since they had known each other, she always turned to him in moments of crisis; he just wished that sometimes she'd share her joys as well. Poor Hannah just seemed to court death and disaster. First that Caroline girl and now Liz Rayman. And he too had known Liz, through Hannah.

Hannah pulled away. "I must smell awful – I've thrown up that many times."

James smiled. "Believe me I've seen and smelled worse today." He wiped his hands over his tired face and exhaled deeply. His fingers rubbed against the stubble.

"James, I'm so sorry. You must be shattered. I just…"

"Don't worry. What are friends for?" His smile was tinged by his own sadness.

Hannah felt the tears well up again.

"Do you have a photo of Liz?"

Hannah nodded. "Why?"

"Could you get one for me?"

"Well I don't have to look far. There's one of us together over there on the mantlepiece."

James stood up and retrieved it. The photograph captured the two friends toasting each other at some party. They both looked so relaxed and happy. Hannah's auburn curls tumbling over her shoulders; Liz's straight dark hair cut into a bob with a heavy fringe. It was taken pre-Elizabeth and they both looked so appealing and attractive in their different ways. Hannah still was. He sat down next to her again.

"Look at Liz here, Hannah. This is how you need to remember her. Keep this photo with you and every time you see that image of Liz tonight, look at this one. Okay?"

"Okay." Hannah tried to smile but her lips felt dry and taut.

"Oh I nearly forgot – I brought you these." He handed her a small pharmaceutical bottle. "It's a sedative to help you relax and sleep."

Hannah took it and rolled the bottle in her hand.

James looked ill-at-ease, his professional "bedside manner" had deserted him.

"Can I get you anything?"

Hannah shook her head. Her mouth tasted distinctly unpleasant. She could smell vomit. She must have spashed herself earlier. Her hair smelled strange as though it had absorbed all the evil that had been in that room. She hadn't eaten since lunchtime and her stomach was gripped in an acidic battle. But the thought of food made her heave.

"I think I'll just have a shower and then go to bed. Thank so much for being here James. I don't know…" Tears dripped down her face and she sniffed.

"Would you like me to stay? Just until you've got yourself into bed?"

"No really –" Hannah looked down at her hands so he wouldn't see the anguish and longing in her eyes. "You just get home now. You must be exhausted."

"Never too tired for a friend." He smiled and looked around in a way Hannah couldn't fathom, then hugged her. It felt so good to be in the safety of his arms. He pulled away.

"Take care and ring me if you need anything. Anything, okay?"

Hannah nodded. She saw him to the door and double locked it before making for the bathroom. She stripped off her clothes and stood under the shower giving vent to her grief until eventually she felt clean enough to go to bed.

"So Sergeant, enlighten me if you will, why did you interview a witness to a horrific murder, in situ, when she was obviously distressed and maybe needing medical attention?"

Mike Benton ran a finger under the collar of his shirt. At that moment he positively hated DI Claudia Turner. Immaculate as ever. She always appeared well groomed and fresh whatever the time of day or night. Now, she looked as though she wanted to have him roasted alive.

"Did she need a medic?"

"She was throwing up in front of you. Don't you ever think?" Turner glanced out of the window. The London nightscape of light and darkness. She sighed thinking about the call she'd taken from Tom Jordan – voice full of concern and underneath something she might have described as fear if she hadn't known better.

"Hannah Weybridge is a journalist on *The News*."

Benton felt his stomach contract. *Shit!* "Guv, I'm sorry… I just thought …"

"You just didn't think, that's your trouble." She looked down at a sheet of paper on her desk. Her next words threw him. "What's happening to you Mike? Don't answer –" she added as he did a fair impression of a goldfish. "Go home. Eat. Sleep. And be ready to make an early start tomorrow."

Sergeant Benton scapped his chair back and noticed the DI wince. "Sorry Guv. Night."

DI Turner nodded and drummed her fingernails on the desk. So who are you really, Hannah Weybridge? She had run a check and come up with a security block. And what was Tom Jordan's connection with her?

Hannah woke at two in the morning. For a moment she was lost in her dream, trying to snatch back the feeling of peace. It was no good. She saw Liz's lifeless body. Was there something about her that was attracting death? Violent death? After everything that had happened with Caroline and that vile Lacon man, she was beginning to think she was cursed.

She turned the pillow over and pulled the duvet up over her face, muffling her sobs, but the horror of the evening before hovered over her. Menacingly. She was chilled to the core of her being. Sleep was elusive. She got up, wrapped herself in a heavy dressing-gown and tip-toed into Elizabeth's room.

From the glow of the nightlight she made out her daughter's beautiful face, eyes tightly closed, lashes caressing her chubby cheeks. Sleeping soundly she looked angelic. Hannah remembered her father's words when Elizabeth was born.

"You feel like no one else in the world could possibly love their child as much as you do, don't you?" That was exactly it. And he had felt it too. With her. She had felt blessed and cherished.

Now she felt lost and alone. Tom hadn't rung back. They had been together for so short a time it now seemed unreal. What did she feel about him? He had made her feel special and cossetted.

Once they had stopped being at cross purposes after the Caroline affair, they had found interests in common and she loved the way her body responded to his touch. The joy of sitting wrapped in each other's arms in silence. No words necessary. Sometimes he only had to look at her and she would get that tingly feeling in her abdomen... But then he went away. New York. What was that all about? A few days together at Christmas was all that they'd had. And that was at her parents' house in the Loire where they'd all celebrated Elizabeth's first birthday. Liz had called and sang happy birthday to an enchanted one year old. It had been a joyful and relaxed time but all too brief. It seemed no sooner had he arrived, than Tom was leaving.

What was so important in New York? A good career move he'd said and it was only a job swap for a few months. But those months seemed agonisingly long. And she needed him with her now.

But she also needed to get a grip. For Elizabeth's sake most of all. She wanted to pick her up, embrace and draw comfort from her. But that was selfish. She had to be the grown up here. She returned to her empty bed.

The next morning Hannah was still in her dressing-gown when Janet arrived.

"Don't take your coat off." Janet looked confused until Hannah added, "Would you mind popping across the road to the newsagent and buying all the papers?" She handed Janet some money which she had ready. Elizabeth, sitting on her hip reached out for the notes and Janet tickled her under her arm making the toddler shriek in delight.

"Right won't be a minute."

Hannah knew that news of Liz's death would have made the later editions. What she didn't know was how much information the police would have released.

Janet's face looked grim when she returned. "Are you really sure you want to read these, Hannah?"

"They can't be any worse for me than seeing my best friend's murdered body." She realised she sounded harsh. "I didn't mean that so sound quite the way it did. Sorry."

Janet just touched her arm lightly. "It's okay. Look, I know it's cold out there but if we dress you up warmly, how about a trip to the park Elizabeth? If that's ok with you Hannah?"

"Of course." She handed over her daughter and went into the sitting room. She could hear Elizabeth's giggles as Janet got her ready. They both appeared round the door to say goodbye.

"Bye bye darling. Have a lovely time."

She heard the front door close behind them and turned her attention to the newspapers. One look at the headlines made her head for the kitchen for some coffee.

"Do-gooder dentist found dead"

"The price of kindness – death"

"Death in Decay"

In fact the headlines were bolder than the story that followed which in all the papers was a brief outline of Liz Rayman's "mission" at St John's, the fact that she had practice in the Barbican and had recently returned from working with a medical charity in Somalia. She had been found by "a friend". Her. She'd found her.

There were one or two quotes from the bystanders Hannah had seen as she had left the church the previous evening and that was that. For the time being at least. Nothing from the vicar who had persuaded her to work there in the first place.

The police were following several lines of enquiry. Oh yes, thought Hannah, and what were they? She wasn't sure she really wanted to know.

Hannah had been six months pregnant when Liz told her of her plans to volunteer in Somalia. Liz would have preferred to tell her when other people were around in the hope it would have a calming effect on Hannah. But that was not to be. Hannah opted for the comfort of her own home when they met.

"But why? Why now?" Hannah was aghast at what she saw as her friend's desertion. She could feel her eyes welling and blinked rapidly.

"I just feel it's the right time for me."

Not for me, Hannah thought but didn't dare say it. Liz had made this decision and although she didn't think her friend should have consulted her about it beforehand, she did think she'd have had some inkling. Had she been so wrapped up in herself she hadn't noticed?

"My Barbican practice almost runs itself now and I have a good team there. What's the point of being the boss, if you can't take a sabbatical. And I need a change..." Liz smiled but Hannah couldn't reciprocate.

"I need you here, Liz, do you have to go so far away?" Hannah knew she sounded like a petulant child but couldn't stop herself.

"Yes, I do. I've been thinking about it for a long time and I'm sorry I won't be here when you have the baby but you do have other friends, Hannah. I can't run my life to your timetable."

If she hadn't known Liz better, Hannah would have been affronted by that comment. But she knew their closeness could be claustophobic. If the roles were reversed, she knew what she would do. Or did she?

"I know, I'm sorry. What did your mother say?"

Liz laughed. "One mountain at a time, Hannah. That's tomorrow's task. To be honest, I'm more worried about what Mary will say."

"Why? She's your mother's companion, not your keeper."

Liz gave her a strange look and sipped her wine. Hannah, because of her condition, wasn't drinking. "Oh I suppose she's just protective of Mummy. When I was younger I always used to confide in Mary first and we'd work out a way to break the news to her. She's really a member of the family and I don't have many of those."

Both Liz's parents had few family connections. Lady Rayman, like her daughter, was an only child. Lord Rayman's two older brothers had both been killed during the war, both fighter pilots. Lord Rayman, who had not expected to accede to the title, had worked for the Home Guard. He had disappeared when Liz was a child and she rarely spoke about him.

"Do you ever wonder about what happened to your father?" Hannah made a face as she drank her non-alcoholic wine. She pushed it away and got up to get a glass of water from the kitchen.

"What do you think?" Liz replied when Hannah returned. "No one likes the idea that something or someone was so much more important in your father's life than you. It's shitty but I've got used to it. No one is indispensable not even fathers." It sounded as though Liz had rehearsed those words.

"Well, I hope that's true for my baby's sake."

"No news from Paul then?"

"No and to be honest I really don't want anything to do with him. Abortion and me or baby without me isn't an ultimatum I'd have expected. Still…" She stroked her bump and Liz watched her friend's face transcend her anger and radiate her love for the unborn child. She felt a pang of raw envy which surprised her. Going to Somalia was definitely the right decision. And she had reasons to go there that she couldn't confide in anyone. Especially not Hannah who tended to react emotionally at the drop of a hat these days. Hormones – and her own weren't always that stable either.

"It's something I need to do, Hannah. Like you and the baby. I'm not deserting you but I am doing what I think is right and important for me. And at the moment that means volunteering in Somalia."

Hannah sniffed back her tears and hugged Liz.

"Just don't be away for too long. I need you here"

"And what about my needs, Hannah?"

Hannah just stared. A tear welled at the corner of her eye but did not fall. "I'm sorry. I'm just being selfish. Forgive me?"

The two women hugged each other tightly but neither forgave the other. Liz departed for Somalia not long afterwards.

THREE

"You know you do have other friends, Hannah. People who love and need you too." Linda smiled but that did not rob her words of their sharpness. She tucked a strand of hair that had escaped her pony tail behind her ear. Dressed in jeans and a jumper that looked as though it could have been her husband's, her demeanour was relaxed but the expression on her face was every bit the school teacher she was, telling off a recalcitrant pupil and brooking no discension.

Hannah was jolted out of her torpor by the tone of her voice and the stern look. "I'm sorry..?"

Linda was aware that the cloak of grief Hannah had wrapped herself in was threatening to overwhelm her. Sometimes it seemed disproportionate.

"Look I know it must have rated as one of if not the worst experience of your life but you do have to move on. Grief has to be worked through, you mustn't cling on to it."

"I wasn't aware that I am 'clinging on to it.'"

Linda could hear the inverted commas around the phrase.

But she wasn't going to let that stop her now. "Hannah there are friends who are here for you. I can't understand why you are not doing something – anything. You are so resourceful – go for it. Help find out who did this to Liz or at least try to make some sense of it. You're a journalist, for God's sake. Write about it. And you need to think of Elizabeth. She needs her mummy."

"She has me." Hannah glanced down at the toddler sleeping in her arms. She felt heavy and secure. A slight bubble appeared between her lips as she exhaled. Her dark lashes caressed her adorable face like butterflies. One chubby little hand clasped Hannah's thumb. She was warm and smelled of milk and the strawberries she'd eaten earlier, a little bud of red at the corner of her mouth. "She has me," Hannah repeated.

"Then make sure you're the best you, you can be." Linda licked her fingers after squeezing a lime into the sauce she was making. The scent lingered in the warm atmosphere of the kitchen above the odours of roasting chicken. Linda topped up their wine glasses. "This is tough love, Hannah. You need to listen. It's appalling what's happened to Liz but it isn't your fault. Her death may be a freak coincidence and happening so soon after what happened, nearly happened with that awful shit of a man is terrible. But you are stronger than this. You've got to be." Linda turned away and stirred the sauce. The wooden spoon lingered in the pan and she stared at it as though it would reveal the secrets of the universe.

"I know I have to do something." Hannah stroked her daughter's arm. "I just feel so powerless. I have no energy for anything."

"That's a natural reaction but you need to fight it."

"Fight what?" David walked into the kitchen holding his son's hand and craddling their four-month-old daughter, Ella, in his arms. He dropped a kiss on the top of Hannah's head. "How's my favourite hack, then."

Linda kissed the latest addition to their family before David placed Ella into her bouncy seat which was then put inside a playpen – added protection against the skirmishes of her older brother.

"Lethargic and underemployed." Hannah ruffled Joel's curls. "However it's a situation I have been told to rectify. And I shall. But on a full stomach." She smiled at Linda. She was right of course but she felt so lonely especially seeing David and Linda together, a vision of domestic harmony.

"Glad to hear it. Heard from Tom lately?"

Hannah caught the furious glance Linda had shot at him. "No. I think that's part of the problem." Elizabeth opened her eyes and stared fixedly for a moment before beaming at her mother and pulling herself up to survey the scene.

"Jo-jo," she squealed in delight and pulled away from the maternal embrace to slide down her legs and hug her little playmate. Hannah wished her own life could be so uncomplicated.

"I really like Tom and thought we had something going for us. But his going off to the States like that… well it's not very flattering is it?" Hannah sipped her wine and missed the look exchanged between David and Linda. "I wasn't looking for a relationship but it just happened and now I don't know where I am, in any part of my life."

"Well right now you are here with us about to have a delicious lunch over which we'll think about life and what to do next." David patted Linda on her bottom and moved to the fridge for another bottle of wine just as Elizabeth let out an almighty shriek. Joel had a clump of her hair in his hand and was tugging for all he was worth.

"No Joel. That's not kind is it?" Gently Linda unclasped his hand and Elizabeth waddled over to her mother and thrust her wet face onto her skirt. Hannah picked her up and kissed the red patch on her scalp just as Joel rushed over and hugged Elizabeth before biting her cheek and leaving a deep red mark. Elizabeth screamed.

"Come on old chap, think we need some cool down time." David lifted the child away and walked out of the room with him.

"Oh Hannah – I'm sorry about that. I don't know what just got into him." She sighed. "Well I do – sibling bloody rivalry rearing its ugly head."

"They're not siblings." Hannah felt a double blow. She adored Linda's firstborn but hated seeing her own child at the mercy of his ourtburst.

"No but he knows he shouldn't hurt the baby – probably wants to kill her – so takes it out on Elizabeth. Shit."

Hannah looked at her friend properly. She looked tired and sad. She put Elizabeth down on the floor then handed Linda her glass. "Nothing to fall out over especially when you were managing to give me such a hard time yourself." Hannah smiled and hugged her friend who blew her nose noisily.

"Okay let's get this food on the table. I'm eating for two still."

Afterwards, back in her own home Hannah thought about what Linda had said. She knew her friend only had her best interests at heart. She had to get a grip. No one was going to do that for her. Liz was dead and nothing she could do would alter the fact but she could try to find out why. And a good place to start would be at the editorial meeting she was due at the next morning. Maybe the news desk would have some leads or at least give her some backup for her own enquiries. The police had been remarkably quiet. Please God there wouldn't be another cover up.

FOUR

"Right, anything on the dead dentist?"

Silence, followed by a few embarrassed coughs, met this statement. Terry Cornhill, the deputy editor who was sitting in for the editor, Georgina Henderson, looked up over his half moon glasses. He looked every inch an absent-minded academic with his shock of white hair, lean body and a rather eccentric sense of fashion – one day a pinstripe suit, the next a hand-knitted jumper that had seen better days – but he was a tabloid journalist to the core with newsprint running through his veins and the nose for a good story. Today he was wearing a fair isle waistcoat that looked as though it had its provenance in the forties.

"I'm sorry Hannah, no offence."

Hannah could feel eight pairs of eyes resting on her. Shortly after her exposé of the group behind the murders of prostitutes at King's Cross had been spiked, she'd been offered – and accepted – a retainer at *The News* and was invited to editorial conferences every few weeks. She was tolerated rather than accepted. But the monthly fee was worth it. With Elizabeth to bring up on her own, any high minded ideals she might have cherished, had had to take a back seat. However it soon became obvious even to her that the contract she'd signed effectively stopped her working for anyone else. She had been spiked again. Silenced. And she had walked into their trap.

"I'd like to cover this story if I may?" she said tentatively.

"Don't you think it's a bit too close to home, dear?" Judy Burton's smile and saccharin tone did nothing to mask the malice in her eyes. Getting the human interest stories had been her province before miss butter-wouldn't-melt arrived and she was not a woman who thrived on competition. Particularly not from a freelance who had no real newspaper experience. And especially not from a freelance whose large retainer or the reason for it was all rather a mystery to the staff journos.

"No I don't." Hannah looked directly at Terry Cornhill. "I was there just after it happened. I know... I knew Liz Rayman and I know her family. I want to find out who killed her and I just don't accept the police version that some tramp – probably drunk or drugged – went berserk and ..."

"Why not?" Rory the news editor was watching her closely.

"For one thing –" Hannah's voice had risen perilously high. She coughed and took a deep breath deliberately lowering her pitch. "For one thing, the people she treated respected her."

"Down and outs, tramps and whores," someone muttered.

"Being homeless and poor doesn't make someone a murderer. There was no reason to kill her. I want to make some sense of her death. I..."

Hannah realised she'd lost everyone's attention if she'd ever had it. Her cheeks burned. She'd said too much yet again. Or rather she hadn't said enough – she hadn't been objective, cool. She'd let everyone see her hurt but not her professionalism, her...

"Okay Hannah." Terry's voice broke into her thoughts. "The story's yours. We'll have a first person account of what it was like to find a close friend murdered. Write that first then get some angle on the priest and see if you can get a few of her clients to talk. Liaise closely with Rory. Right that's it folks. Hang on a minute Rory, will you? And you too Jude."

The phone was ringing as Hannah unlocked the front door and stopped abruptly as she rushed up the stairs. From behind the study door she could hear her own voice asking the caller to leave a message or to contact her on her mobile phone. Hannah dived into the room and picked up the receiver.

"Hello this is Hannah Weybridge."

"Oh Hannah, thank goodness. I do so hate leaving messages on those machines. Liz always..." The well modulated tones of Celia Rayman broke off. Hannah could visualise the older woman's delicately made up face and elegantly groomed, steel grey hair. That was how she always looked but that was before Liz's death. Maybe now Celia looked lined and haggard, her eyes haunted...

"I'm so sorry dear, I still can't get used to..." Liz's mother paused searching for a word to describe her daughter's violent departure from the world. There was none.

"Neither can I, Celia, I..."

"Look dear, let's not talk on the phone, it's so difficult and I ... and I..."

The sob of desperation she could hear in Celia's voice brought tears to Hannah's own eyes. She swallowed hard.

"Could you come over to see me, Hannah? This afternoon? And bring that adorable baby of yours."

"Well if you're sure?" Hannah was referring to Elizabeth's inclusion in the invitation. Celia Rayman had been forthright in her opinions when she had heard that Hannah was pregnant and intended to bring up a child on her own. It was surprising really since, after her husband had inexplicably walked out on her when Liz was just three years old, Celia had in effect been a single parent. Robert Rayman had never been seen or heard of again and his deserted wife had long since given up making any reference to him.

"She'll do me the power of good," the older woman continued. "Would two-thirty suit you?"

Hannah smiled. That was the old Celia. Always asking if a time would suit when you knew damn well it would inconvenience her greatly if you didn't accept her schedule.

"That'll be fine, Celia. I'll see you then."

If Hannah had expected a distraught and weeping mother made inarticulate by the sudden loss of her only child, she was in for a shock. Celia Rayman bore no outward signs of her grief. She did not look haggard, dishevelled. She appeared as immaculate as ever. Her white hair was caught back in its customary chignon, her nose was powdered and her lips defined with their usual pink lustre. If anything her eyes seemed colder, harder. But her expression softened when Hannah and Elizabeth were shown into the drawing-room of the large Kensington house the Raymans had owned for ever.

"Hannah!" Celia walked over to them her arms outstretched. Her cheeks made momentary contact with Hannah's but for the first time in their acquaintance, the younger woman felt the older's firm embrace.

Celia stepped back. Her eyes looked suspiciously aqueous but she turned her gaze to the toddler. Hannah was amazed by the tenderness of her smile. Celia knelt down.

"Hello Elizabeth. How lovely to see you. Come over here and I'll show you what I've found for you to play with."

With no hesitation Elizabeth clasped the proffered hand and waddled over to the sofa where there was a collection of cuddly animals, some of which must have once have been dearly loved judging from their battered and threadbare condition. Liz's? Hannah had to press her fingernails into her palms. She couldn't, wouldn't break down in front of Celia.

Elizabeth was happily playing with and rearranging the soft toys when tea and coffee arrived on a tray which was placed on the highly polished table at Celia's side by her companion and housekeeper of many years standing. Mary Cuthrington smiled tremulously at Hannah, looked to be about to say something then left the high ceilinged room quickly but not as silently as she might have wished. Hannah glanced at Celia who made no comment on the receding figure.

"I remembered you don't drink tea, my dear." Hannah was touched. Although the older woman was certainly grief-stricken, she maintained her role.

The niceties over and Elizabeth chatting away to the teddies in some make-believe world, Celia turned her attention to Hannah. Without preamble she began, "I don't believe for one moment that my daughter was killed by some ... some... " Celia's hand shook as she took another sip of tea. "Some drunken down and out. There's more to it than that and I want you Hannah to find out for me exactly what was so important that my daughter had to lose her life for it!"

Celia's colour had risen and so had her voice but she was not about to break down. Celia Rayman was far too furious for that. Hannah felt her admiration for the woman she had grown to know through her friendship with Liz increase enormously.

"I'm not sure I understand you."

In the cab going home, with Elizabeth slumbering peacefully in her car seat, Hannah mulled over her conversation with Celia. Her friend's mother had astonished her with the proposal that Hannah should act for her and investigate Liz's death. Celia had been adamant that she would pay Hannah.

"My dear girl you simply cannot afford to be sentimental in this world." They were both silent for a moment. Had Liz lost her life for that emotion? "I phoned around some of these... agencies... and I believe this will cover your time and let me know if you have any expenses."

Hannah's eye's hardly focussed on the cheque or the amount it was made out for but she did agree to meet Celia the next day at Liz's Barbican practice where she also lived "above the shop", very much to Celia's annoyance.

Elizabeth sighed in her sleep and Hannah stroked her cheek. She still couldn't take in Celia's parting comment.

"Of course you knew she was pregnant, didn't you?"

Hannah had felt her world tilt sideways. She was stunned by this revelation. She'd had no idea Liz had been even thinking about having a child. It made Hannah realise how far apart they had grown. How little she now knew of her friend.

What a double tragedy for Celia. The loss of her daughter and her unborn grandchild. No wonder she was angry.

FIVE

Paul Montague stared at the man sitting opposite him. He thought he'd never recognise him again if seen in a crowd. He was nondescript with his grey hair and horn-rimmed spectacles but he exuded an air of menace that made Paul more afraid than he'd ever been before in his entire life. He had never thought of himself as particularly principled but this man was in a league of his own. What he was asking…

"Do I have to make myself any clearer Mr Montague?" The silence stretched between them like an unplayed note on a violin string. "Either you do as we ask or we pull the plug on your company, your assets and your family…".

"My parents are dead," he said as if that fact would save him.

"But not your daughter."

"I don't have a daughter."

"Not what our intelligence leads us to believe. A liaison with a certain Hannah Weybridge … Elizabeth born…"

"You contemptible shit." Paul's collar felt tight, his hands clammy. He'd known when he'd borrowed the money against his house and company that he was taking a risk. But that was how business expansion worked. He hadn't known that the loan company had such dubious or frankly criminal connections. In fact how he'd got into this situation was a mystery. A decidedly scary one.

"How did you come to take over my loan. I wasn't defaulting. There was no problem with repayments." Paul was clutching at straws and he knew it.

The man before him in this pokey, grey office tucked away in a back street of Westminster, smiled. Icy fingers gripped his heart.

"No there was no problem." Again that silence. "We made that company a very generous offer which they didn't refuse. And now I'm making you an offer. A challenge if you like. All you have to do is ingratiate yourself with a certain journalist to find out what we need to know. Piece of cake for a man of your talents surely."

Paul felt like a hooked fish gulping for air.

"What do you need to know?" He tried to keep his voice level but it betrayed his fear. His bespoke suit felt too tight. He undid the jacket button.

"It's all here." He pushed a large manilla envelope towards Paul. "That's the background. Read it at your leisure. We need to know where certain information is or how far it has been disseminated. That's all. Nothing too difficult for a man of your intelligence and connections." That smile would curdle milk.

Paul picked up the envelope and stood up. He felt a trickle of sweat run down the inside of his shirt as he buttoned up his jacket.

"Don't take too long, Mr Montague. Very powerful men are depending on you. Do I make myself clear?"

"You do." Paul made his exit as quickly as he could without appearing to be running scared. Outside the door he put on his coat. It felt heavier than when he went in or maybe it was because he had withered inside. An hour ago he had not known of this man's existence. An hour ago his life was on track. One phone call and a meeting later had put an end to all that.

Then as he walked out of the street door some of his previous confidence returned. He'd just find out whatever these people wanted – if he could – and then he'd be off the hook.

SIX

Celia Rayman sighed, stood up and walked across to the 15th floor window and looked out at the cityscape below. There was St Giles-without-Cripplegate engulfed in a maze of stairways, pedestrian bridges and high buildings. Only a few fountains to distract the eye.

"I've never liked this flat. Never... But I'd give anything to have Liz here now."

Hannah heard the sob in her voice and hesitated. Celia was not the type of woman to encourage physical contact. She stood rigid in her grief and Hannah had to pull her away from the window to the sofa.

"Oh Hannah it's such a waste. Such a loss. I..."

The younger woman embraced the slim frame, stroked her hand and murmured reassuring words much as she would have done if Elizabeth had fallen over and hurt herself.

"What must you think of me?" said Celia pulling away and blowing her nose delicately into a lace-edged handkerchief.

Hannah wiped her eyes with a crumpled tissue. "You're a mother who's lost her only daughter. I can understand that, although I can't begin to imagine how you must feel..."

Celia patted her hand. "Yes, you have dear little Elizabeth. Liz was so delighted when you named her and asked her to be a godmother –" Hannah did not correct the use of the word but Celia interpreted her expression – "sponsor, whatever. It all comes down to the same thing. Now," her voice took on a business-like quality, "the police have taken away a few things but my impression is that they weren't looking for anything really. They still seem convinced Liz was murdered by one of her homeless patients. So I suggest we look for any of her diaries and appointment books and the computer disks. Yours is compatible, I take it?"

Hannah, amused at the technical phrasing, shook her head. "'Fraid not. Mine's a ..."

"Never mind, you'll just have to take the computer too. A nuisance, I know, but needs must."

Hannah glanced around the room Liz used as a study. It was immaculate. Liz had furnished the whole appartment in a minimalist Swedish style and everything was glass and leather. Each of the five rooms was ordered and neat; it looked more like a show house than someone's home. But that was Liz for you. Hannah thought of her own cluttered house and could never imagine her friend leaving a sinkful of washing-up or dirty clothes lying on the bedroom floor.

In fact, like mother like daughter, Celia had already switched on the washing machine when she arrived having stripped the bed. But a little while later, Hannah had found her sitting on the edge of the mattress clutching a blouse to her face, inhaling all that was left of her dead daughter's fragrance.

"I'm going to leave everything else as it is," she said as she made her way through the apartment pulling out plugs and making sure windows were firmly locked. "Anyway it might not be up to me. We haven't had the will read yet."

"But surely..." Hannah was about to say that surely the police had checked the will to see who would benefit from Liz's death. Up until now she'd assumed her mother would inherit everything with perhaps a small bequest to Elizabeth. But as Liz had been pregnant, maybe she had left everything to the putative father.

"Had Liz planned to marry?" she asked gently.

Celia gave her a despairing look. "How should I know? It was the police who told me of her condition. The pregnancy was noted during the post mortem. Eight weeks gestation." Celia's tone was clipped and all at once she looked older than her years. "Perhaps no one else knew. Perhaps she didn't know herself?"

Oh I think she knew, thought Hannah. *I bet that's what she was going to tell me when* ... But who was the father? Liz hadn't had a regular boyfriend for ages. Still... "Had you met any of her boyfriends recently?" Hannah asked.

Celia shook her head. "I think I'll lock up now. I told them we'd be at the surgery at eleven o'clock. We'll leave that –" she pointed to the computer they had carried to the door – "for the porter to bring down."

Hannah rubbed her eyes and swung her chair round away from the scrolls of information on the screen. She stood up and stretched to release the tension in her shoulders. Hannah looked at her watch. For two hours she'd been going through the files on Liz's computer and disks. She needed a break and went downstairs to catch up on the day's news.

She poured herself a glass of wine and just as she switched on the television, the telephone rang. Using the remote to turn the sound down, she settled herself on the sofa, her legs curled beneath her, and picked up the receiver. "Hannah Weybridge."

There was a slight pause before Tom's voice came over like a warm caress. "How are you and how's little Elizabeth?"

"We're fine." Just hearing his voice brought memories. The lump in her throat threatened to put an end to all conversation.

"Hannah..?"

"Oh Tom I've just been through Liz's files and..."

"What the hell for?" Tom sounded perpelexed and irritated although Hannah couldn't think why. She felt affronted.

"Celia, Liz's mother, has asked me to investigate her death." To Hannah's own ears the word investigate linked to her feeble enquiries seemed nothing short of an exaggeration if not a blatant contravention of the trades' description act.

"But Hannah you don't know the first thing about investigating a murder!"

"I'm investigating as a journalist not as a detective and she's paying me. Anyway if you have so little confidence in my capabilities you can give me some tuition." She said this lightly but Tom evidently took her seriously.

"Have you got the results of the post mortem yet?"

"Well I haven't seen the report but apparently Liz died of a massive heart attack presumably brought on by the knife slashing her neck and fear of her assailant." Hannah marvelled that she managed to keep her voice so matter of fact.

"Go on," prompted Tom, the time lapse in the conversation making it seem all the more weird.

"That wound, it appears was not fatal. It seems strange to me though. Liz never had a problem with her heart, with her health in general. One surprise it did reveal is that Liz was eight weeks pregnant."

A noise somewhere between a sigh and a snort emanated from the phone. "Get another one done."

"I'm sorry?"

"Have another, private post mortem carried out," said Tom.

"But why?" To Hannah a post mortem was a post mortem whoever carried it out.

"The pathologist may have missed something. Anyway it pays to be sure..."

"Of what?"

"We'll see." Background sounds suggested someone else had come into the room. "I'll have to ring off now but you take care. And for God's sake don't take any risks. If you discover anything at all go to the police!" The last words were spoken as if underlined.

Hannah mumbled her goodbyes. A second post mortem, that was something positive to get Celia, as next of kin, to arrange. She turned her attention to the television screen but her mind was not engaged. Tom's lack of confidence in her abilities to examine Liz's death reinforced her own worries. She was out of her depth and she knew it. She wanted to phone Celia and release herself from the task but as she watched a film clip of flooding in the north east, it occurred to her that perhaps Celia wanted to use her because, as a friend, she'd be protective of Liz's past life and reputation. And there was nothing to stop Hannah employing professionals to help her.

Feeling easier, Hannah stretched out her legs before almost leaping into an upright position. Filling the screen was the picture of an elderly man with a rather strange expression on his face. Expression aside, there was no denying his identity. The eyes were now opaque but the white leonine hair and craggy features were incontrovertibly those of the man who had asked her what was happening as she left St John's on the night of Liz Rayman's murder. And now he too had been found dead. In suspicious circumstances it would seem. The police were making this appeal to try to trace his family and ascertain his identity via the media.

Hannah felt a rush of adrenaline and a wave of fear. Was there a link between him and Liz? Hannah took the stairs two at a time and within minutes was at her desk again, searching through Liz's index boxes. Liz's regular Barbican patients all had computer files but details of her "missionaries" as she had nicknamed them in her diary were all meticulously logged on lined cards.

Not knowing what to look for or where to begin Hannah started at A. Many of the names seemed in code or so it appeared to Hannah. Albatross, Archimedes, Axel... she sighed, the only way to identify them would be to examine their teeth and match dental records! Well the police could arrange that, she thought, finding the number the policewoman had given her and propping it on the phone to remind her to ring in the morning.

As she stood up, her arm caught the corner of the box file which fell unceremoniously to the floor expelling its contents on the way. As she was about to replace the collected cards, Hannah noticed the bottom of the box wobbled a bit as though something was stuck underneath it. Intrigued – Liz was always so neat and precise about everything – Hannah levered up the base and then almost dropped the box again.

Her gasp rang out in the silent room as the penetrating gaze of the tramp who had been pulled out of the Thames stared up at her.

There had been a dozen or so photographs in the box. But the shock of finding the dead man's image at the top of the pile was almost too much for Hannah. She went downstairs to the kitchen and poured herself a brandy. The amber liquid warmed her throat and Hannah, eyes closed, leaned her back against the cupboard and took some calming breaths. Her heartbeat gradually returned to near-normal and Hannah, glass in hand, returned to her study.

On the reverse of the Polaroid, in Liz's neat hand was written: Jacob Gurnstein 3/8/1931. She sat staring at the photograph as though willing it to reveal more information. None was forthcoming. At least she'd be able to give his name to the police and they could trace his family if he had any.

SEVEN

"Miss Weybridge?" The lilting tones were unknown.

"Ms." Hannah's stock reply.

"I'm sorry, yes of course." A pause. "This is Patrick Ryan here."

"Yes." Hannah tried to keep the edge from her voice. Working from home she received more calls than she cared to count from "financial advisors" and double glazing salesmen offering their services. However this man didn't sound as though he were selling anything.

"Father Patrick Ryan... From St John's... A friend of Liz Rayman." Each piece of information seemed to be wrung from him.

Hannah who hadn't had much contact with priests was uncertain as to how to address him. "What can I do for you – Father?" It was alien to her but that was the title he gave himself.

"Patrick, please. I'd ... I'd like to talk to you." This was followed by a silence which rather belied his words.

Hannah took pity on him. "Would you like to meet?" she offered.

"That would be preferable. Could you come to St John's?"

"I don't know, I don't think..." Immediately the scene of Liz's murder materialised to haunt her.

"The church is very beautiful sacred place. A terrible deed doesn't alter that."

"No but..."

"There's something I must show you Hannah – I'm sorry Liz talked about you so often that I feel I know you. Could you come this afternoon?"

Hannah wondered why everyone should assume she was at their beck and call and had nothing better to do. However she had nothing pressing and confirmed that she could meet that afternoon and, intrigued, hung up. She had always assumed that the priest who ran the soup kitchen would have been eloquent indeed to have involved Liz in his enterprise. This man hardly seemed able to string a sentence together. Maybe he disliked phones. Maybe, said a little voice, it's grief.

Hannah sighed. She'd spent a wasted hour that morning being interviewed by the police. Janet, an immense improvement on the last nanny, had taken Elizabeth off to the park. Now Hannah could hear her chuckling contentedly downstairs. Hannah had planned a couple of hours with her this afternoon but now... Now she had to make do with a big cuddle, she thought as she went downstairs and elicted a delighted squeal from her daughter nestling in her arms. Hannah's mind went over that morning's conversation with Detective Inspector Turner. After the formal introduction, she'd been surprised by her next comment.

"You're a friend of Tom Jordan, aren't you?"

"Yes." Hannah smiled at the thought of the absent Tom. "How did you know? Do you know him?"

DI Turner's smile did not extend beyond her mouth. Her grey eyes looked wary. A forefinger stroked her nose that was lightly dusted in freckles. "We were at Hendon together and our paths have crossed once or twice since then."

Briefly Hannah wondered if they had been lovers. So what if they had? She shouldn't mind but it did niggle. Claudia Turner was immaculately turned out in a dark green linen suit the colour of which complemented her strawberry blond hair. Hannah loved that colour and wondered idly if it were natural. She felt positively shabby beside her.

They were seated in Hannah's sitting room and Claudia's eyes seemed to take in every detail. Hannah smiled to herself. What a difference a few months made. The tattered settee and old armchairs had been replaced with two two-seater green leather Chesterfields. Hannah loved them and they really "lifted" the room. And, of course she'd had to have the room completely redecorated after the fiasco with Gerry Lacon. Fiasco was a word she used to rob the incident of the power to reduce her to a nervous wreck. He had been going to shoot Elizabeth.

Hannah shivered as Claudia had had to remove a doll before she could sit down and she was obviously not amused when the officer with her admired one of Elizabeth's brick constructions. Hannah offered coffee which was declined and then produced the box-file and the photograph of Jacob Gurnstein.

"I couldn't find a corresponding card for him," explained Hannah. "Liz Rayman seems to have kept Polaroids of most of her clients at St John's. Presumably because they all appear to give one name only. Apparently there's a preponderance of Arnies in Waterloo." Hannah smiled. The detective who'd been introduced as DC Shaw coughed – sympathetically Hannah thought – into the silence which followed this remark.

"And how do you come to be in possession of these, Ms Weybridge?"

Hannah could almost touch the animosity directed at her. Probably she just didn't like journalists. She was presumably also peeved that her officers hadn't found the box file, or if they had, hadn't checked it thoroughly.

"Lady Celia Rayman –" Hannah emphasised the title that the bearer rarely used – "asked me to go through her daughter's files."

"Why?" The inspector held her gaze.

Hannah looked straight into those hostile eyes. "I am a friend of the family and Lady Rayman is not computer literate."

"But these were not on the computer."

"I am sure, Inspector Turner, you'll appreciate a mother's distress at her daughter's death," she said icily.

Turner brushed an imaginary speck from her skirt. *That's how she regards me*, thought Hannah, *as something to be brushed away.* "But you're rather quick off the mark, aren't you?"

Hannah didn't wince but she paused to bite back a scathing retort. "Liz Rayman was a professional woman, Inspector, with a private practice and employees. Decisions, however painful and in your eyes premature, have to be made. Other people's lives and livelihoods are affected by this tragedy."

"Quite." Claudia Turner stood up. "Well thank you for your time, Ms Weybridge. We'll keep this for the time being – it's a better likeness. We'll be in touch." She made the words sound like a threat.

"How did he die?" Hannah asked as she saw them to the door.

"We're not sure yet," said DC Shaw. "But it looks like suicide. His body was found in the Thames."

"Looks like he murdered your friend then topped himself," volunteered the inspector.

"Why? Why would he kill her and then himself?"

Turner stared hard at her for a moment. "What's the matter, Ms Weybridge? Not a glamorous enough death for your friend? Do you need something more sensational for *The News*. Sorry to disappoint you," she sneered.

Hannah was stunned. She couldn't think why the woman was so antagonistic towards her and at the same time she didn't for one minute believe that Jacob Gurnstein had killed Liz and then himself. It just didn't add up. She hadn't told them she'd seen Jacob on the night of the murder. They'd probably say killers always return to the scene of crime or some other such received wisdom. If it had to come out some time she'd say she had been confused and only remembered later. Evidently the police thought this was an open and shut case.

"So you'll be closing this particular matter quite soon then?" Hannah asked innocently.

"That's really none of you business is it?" came the charming reply.

"I didn't for one minute think it was," commented Hannah more to herself than the backs disappearing down her short front path. How fortunate she'd thought to have had a copy of the photograph made earlier that morning.

Hannah looked across the road and saw Leah Braithwaite making bin emptying into an activity akin to painting the Forth Bridge. Hannah pretended not to see her neighbour's wave and eager expression and shut the door firmly.

February 1993

Just had a letter – much delayed – from Hannah. The baby, a girl, has arrived and she is ecstatic. Wish I could feel the same. Of course I'll make all the right noises and say how delighted I am that she is named after me and how wonderful to be a "sponsor".

I don't feel that. I am jealous right to the core of my being. Living in this horrendous place and trying to make a difference has exhausted me. Much tougher than being a single mum, Hannah!

What she ever saw in Paul I'll never know. But no accounting… And there was a time when… he made a pass at me and I was tempted. Well more than that. It did become "almost sex" if you can call it that. Thank heavens I saw reason in time. Especially as it was only a week later that Hannah told me she was pregnant. Paul must have known then. Bastard.

Hannah included a photo. Baby Elizabeth looks cute but don't all babies?

I hate the way I'm feeling now. So glad I don't have to be there and pretend. It would have been so difficult to act …

Act what?

I want a child. Life can be so unfair. What's wrong with me that I can't get myself a husband or at least a partner to procreate with.

Not much choice here, either. Sam Lockwood is a lovely man. Committed. Educated and intelligent. Some of the others leave a lot to be desired. John has gone native… Vicky the only other woman here keeps herself to herself. Much like me I suppose.

I despair of ever finding Kamaria. A beautiful name "like the moon" for such a beautiful child. Sometimes I hope she's dead. Otherwise her present is too awful to contemplate. How can a young girl cope with being torn from her family, multiple rapes … Yes I pray she's dead.

EIGHT

Hannah had changed out of her jeans and had donned a dress and jacket for her appointment with the priest. Having a regular income now meant she had been able to spend some money on her wardrobe and had a few smart outfits. The clothes gave her a confidence she often didn't feel. Today was no exception.

She had mixed feelings about going back to the scene of Liz's death and as the mini-cab drew up outside the church she had a strong compunction to tell the driver to take her back home.

However, bathed in winter sunlight, the church took on a different hue and, as she stepped through the huge wooden doors that stood open, she felt an unusual sense of peace flow over her. In the distance the faint sounds of an organ, then the loud peel of the three o'clock bell.

Hannah had been looking up at the intricate stained glass window depicting Christ and two disciples, and almost jumped out of her skin when a figure cloaked in black spoke her name in tones which seemed to echo into infinity.

She stepped forward. "Father Ryan?"

"Patrick, please." He took her hand and his eyes held hers. His penetrating gaze was disconcerting. There was an animal sensuality about him that Hannah found hard to reconcile to her idea of a priest. At the same time there was something she couldn't quite put her finger on that made her shiver.

He indicated that they should walk towards the altar. "It must have been a terrible shock for you to discover Liz like that."

That was an understatement. "Yes."

"I blame myself, of course." Father Patrick didn't seemed inclined to elaborate.

"Why – because you persuaded her to run a surgery?"

Patrick Ryan said nothing. His face bore all the signs of a man tormented by immense grief.

"Surely you don't believe that one of her patients killed her do you?"

"I don't know what to think."

Hannah was beginning to lose patience. "Why was Liz left to run her clinic alone here. Surely it makes sense to have someone else in the vicinity?"

"Of course." Patrick's hand went to the large silver cross that rested on his chest. "I was here…"

"What? You certainly weren't here when I arrived."

"No I was called away. An emergency at St Thomas's." He ran his fingers through his hair. "Anyway it was a false alarm. When I got there the patient – supposedly one of my parishioners – had been discharged. By the time I got back here, there was police tape everywhere and I wasn't allowed in. I'm so sorry."

For a moment they were both absorbed in their own thoughts. It occurred to Hannah that he could have been deliberately enticed away from the church. But she didn't give vent to that idea as they moved ever nearer to the altar.

"Did you know Jacob Gurnstein?"

They had reached the two steps up into the sanctuary; Patrick had genuflecteed, crossed himself then turned to sit in one of the chairs.

"Who?" Father Ryan did not seem to be paying much attention to her.

"Jacob Gurnstein. He was fished out to the river yesterday and the police seem to think he was Liz's killer."

"Jacob?" Patrick looked at her with unseeing eyes. "Dead?"

"I'm sorry – " Hannah touched his arm – "I didn't realise you didn't know..."

"Why should you?" Hannah felt the full impact of his smile which was so sudden she felt confused.

"You said you had something to show me?" Hannah prompted.

Father Ryan had the grace to look sheepish. "I'm afraid I've got you here under false pretences." He was silent for so long Hannah wondered if he were praying or calculating how to get her on his side. "I needed to see you," he said simply.

Patrick Ryan put down the telephone receiver and sat at his leather topped desk with his head in his hands. His long, lean fingers interwoven in to his thick curly hair which was saved from being described as mousy by the blondish highlights which looked totally natural.

It was, one could say, a masculine room. There was an upright piano and a whole wall of shelves which contained books, a collection of CDs and videos, a stereo system which looked expensive to Hannah's uninitiated eye. The curtains were crimson, heavy velvet and everything had a clean and polished hue. The house was in Roupell Street just behind St John's where all the front doors opened directly onto the street. It belonged to the church, Patrick had said as if justifying his occupancy. It was not a typical vicarage.

The telephone had rung as they entered the sitting room that doubled as the priest's study. Now Patrick turned to her, his face distorted by what she first took to be grief but what soon transpired to be fury.

"Someone, Hannah, is trying to blackmail me."

NINE

Hannah hardly glanced at the vehicle parked outside the house. It was unknown to her. Not that that was unusual in London. Added to which, she had a total blind spot when it came to cars. Most of her friends' and neighbours' cars she recognised by shape or colour. Her old friend Joe had been incensed when she had failed to notice he had a new, more expensive company car. And once she'd been describing the rather sporty red car owned by a man who had taken her out when Liz let out a shriek, "But Hannah that's a Porsche!" Clearly she, if not Hannah, had been impressed.

This car looked sporty too. Maroon. What was that supposed to say about the driver she wondered during the few seconds it took to turn the key in the front door.

Voices greeted her instantly and Hannah felt her stomach tighten into a ball. She hated people arriving when she wasn't there. She was fiercely protective of both her child and her home – more so since Caroline – and she wondered what could have possessed Janet, who had been given very precise instructions when she had been taken on, to allow someone in.

As she walked into the sitting room the polite, social smile she had fixed on her face froze. The man, looking so at home on her leather sofa, stood up.

"Hannah..." he said contriving to sound diffident but as Hannah knew well he hardly lacked confidence. Paul Montague always got what he wanted. Nearly always, Hannah corrected herself. He had not managed to persuade Hannah to have an abortion. "It's me or the baby Hannah," he had said. "You can't have both." And he smiled in a way which suggested that there was no competition. He was right but not in the way he had imagined.

Hannah swallowed hard. She hadn't seen Paul for nearly two years and he was the last person she wanted to see right now. The moment seemed to go on for ever but it was probably only a few seconds before Elizabeth waddled over, beaming.

"Mama..." Elizabeth clutched her monther's legs.

Kneeling down Hannah wrapped her arms around the small body taking comfort from her familiar fragrance, the softness of her skin. She would have loved to hide behind her as she wished away the scene before her.

"Hello darling," she said nuzzling her neck. "Will you go upstairs with Janet to run your bath? I shan't be long."

Elizabeth looked as though she was about to protest with a shriek but did take Janet's hand as the nanny, obeying the cue, led her away.

"Nice girl," Paul murmured as Hannah closed the door after them. She wasn't quite sure which "girl" he was referring to.

"What the hell are you doing here Paul?"

Paul had sat down again. "I would have thought that was obvious. I've come to see you, of course."

"Why?" None of the reasons that sprang to Hannah's mind was acceptable.

"I was in the area – " he shrugged. "I just thought I'd drop in. See how you're faring." His gaze took in the room and Hannah's frock and smart boots. He smiled that old smile which once had made Hannah's stomach turn somersaults but now left her strangely immune. That, at least, was a relief.

"You look well. You both do."

"We are." Hannah still hadn't sat down. "I won't ask you how you are because frankly I really don't care. What I do care about is why you are here?"

"I told you, I..."

"Rubbish. I haven't heard from you for nearly two years. You didn't even bother to find out about the baby.... When you departed, that was it. And you conveniently changed your business and home addresses in case I tried to contact you."

"Did you?" He looked pleased. "Did you try to contact me?"

"No Paul I did not. If I'd wanted to find you, rest assured I would have found it no problem." Her tone would have frozen sand in the Sahara.

Paul was silent for a moment. "I can see my visit's come as a shock," he conceded. "I thought you'd be pleased to see me." He tried to look crestfallen but didn't quite manage it. "I'll go now but I'll talk to you soon." He smiled. "Elizabeth is my daughter too, remember."

Hannah felt faint. She took a deep breath and steadied herself against the door she was holding open for him. "Elizabeth has been your 'daughter' for the past 14 months. You, however, gave up any rights in that department a long time ago."

"Did I?" He spoke quietly but there was no mistaking the undertone of menace in his voice. He picked up his car keys which he'd left on the table, a habit which had always irritated Hannah throughout their five year relationship, and sauntered out. "I'll be in touch."

They were the last words Hannah wanted to hear. She shut the front door firmly behind him before running up the stairs and barging into the bathroom. "Never – ever –" the words almost exploded from her – "let anyone into my house again when I'm not here. I thought I'd made that perfectly clear when I took you on."

Janet's face reddened. "But... but he said..."

"I don't care what he said. No one comes in, is that understood?" Hannah knew she was being unreasonable. Paul's charm could be devastating when he chose. She had no doubt that he'd managed to overcome any reservations Janet had had.

A cry from Elizabeth diverted her attention. She knelt down by the bath, picked up a small duck and made ridiculous quacking sounds until the toddler was giggling and had blown bubbles onto her mother's face.

Janet had busied herself picking up the discarded clothes. Her face was very pink and just for the moment Hannah wondered if she was about to cry. That was all she needed now. "Janet, why don't you go and load the washing machine and tidy up downstairs?" She smiled in what she hoped was a conciliatory manner as the girl, obviously glad to escape, left the bathroom.

Another abortive call out. Father Patrick headed down York Road towards the Bull Ring and St John's. He wrapped his cloak more tightly around him to ward off the bitter chill in the air. The weather did little to improve his mood. The ward sister at St Thomas's, Mary O'Callaghan, had been adamant that no one had asked to see him and even checked with the hospital chaplain.

"Not that we're not always happy to see you, Father. Will I get you a cup of tea before you leave."

Patrick had been persuaded to join Mary for tea and biscuits in her office and and made the most of warming up before leaving.

The tea had not dissipated his irritation. This was the second time recently he'd been called to the hospital under false pretences – to visit a non-existent patient. His mind went back to the first occasion. The evening Liz Rayman was murdered. And he had left her there alone and vulnerable.

Now it occurred to him that his absence was orchestrated by someone who wanted Liz dead. Like her friend Hannah, he didn't believe for one moment that she had been killed by one of her homeless patients. She had been killed for what she knew and he was being blackmailed for the same reason.

He crossed the road and descended into the underpass. Two men jostled him.

"Sorry, Father."

His arms were being held from both sides and he felt a prick at the side of his neck before everything went black.

"Right so how did Paul Montague manage to overide my intructions – my very clear, specific intructions that when I was out of the house no one, no one was allowed to come in?" Hannah had joined the nanny who was packing away toys in the sitting room, Elizabeth looking pink and relaxed after her bath was in her arms.

Janet stared at the floor. When she looked up, her face bore an unreadable expression. Far from being overcome with remorse, Hannah realised that the nanny not only thought she was being unreasonable but that she had done nothing wrong.

Hannah cleared her throat. "You are still here on probation, Janet."

For a split second Hannah thought the younger woman was going to walk out, then something stopped her. An unpleasant thought crossed her mind. Had Paul said something to win her over? Had he offered her some incentive? It seemed improbable. But you could never be too sure. Not when Elizabeth was involved.

"I am sorry, Hannah. He came to the door with an enormous bouquet –" Hannah raised an eyebrow – "the flowers are in the kitchen. And a huge teddy for Elizabeth. He did ask for you first and when I said you were out..." Janet paused. "Come to think of it, he didn't seem surprised you were out. It's as though he expected it..."

"Or knew," said Hannah more to herself than to Janet.

"At first I thought he was an uncle or something but he said he was Elizabeth's father. Then he more or less pushed his way in and –"

"I'll have to do something about security," Hannah muttered.

"What?"

"Nothing. Go on."

"Well he was really only in here a few minutes – ten, fifteen at most – when you came back."

"Did you leave her alone with him?"

"Only to take the flowers to the kitchen. I didn't even put them in water. I came straight back. He was just talking to Elizabeth and she looked quite happy."

A shaft of pure hatred pierced Hannah's heart. She didn't want Paul in their lives. Not now, not ever. He had had his chance and forfeited that right when he walked out after Hannah told him she was pregnant. His parting words today "I'll be back," echoed in her mind.

"Right. I explained when I took you on that there are reasons why I don't want you to let anyone in the house – anyone whoever they may claim to be." She studied Janet's face which was now rather pink. "If that is too much to ask, that you follow my instructions, then..."

TEN

The scene with Paul and then Janet left Hannah feeling even more drained than she'd felt after her conversation with Father Patrick and his astounding claim that he was being blackmailed.

Her mind went back to the scene in his sitting room which doubled as his study.

She had been stunned by his fury when he said, "I'm being blackmailed."

Hannah hadn't known what to say or why he had chosen to tell her. "Isn't there someone in the church hierarchy you can talk to?" Then a terrible thought struck her. "Do you know anything about Liz's murder?"

The priest looked up blankly. Then there was a dawning realisation. "Good God, you don't think I killed her?" He looked as though the very thought would choke him.

Hannah said nothing. She had always found silence a good way to get people to talk. Listening was her strength.

"Perhaps this was a mistake. I should never have asked you to come here... But Liz was always talking about you and how much your friendship meant to her that I... I have assumed too much. I'm sorry."

"Did Liz know you were being blackmailed or has this happened since her ... her death?" Hannah still found that word so hard to pronounce.

Father Patrick studied his hands as though he could see his future written there or at least the words he would say next. He looked up and Hannah could see how much he was struggling not to break down. It seemed rather strange to her. Shouldn't priests be the ones to cope, to understand death? To console and help people through their grief? It made her wonder about his relationship with Liz. Could he be the father of her unborn child? It seemed far-fetched; she couldn't imagine Liz becoming romantically involved with a priest. But there again she hadn't imagined her going off to work with a medical charity in Somalia or coming back and running a drop-in dentist facility either.

Father Patrick loooked up as though he'd come to some sort of decision. "The blackmail started before Liz, before Liz died. But she didn't know anything about it."

Privately Hannah doubted that. "So her murder and your being blackmailed are not connected?"

"I didn't say that."

"What are you saying, Patrick? And really why are you telling me. You should really go to the police."

"I spoke to Lady Rayman yesterday." He said this as though the fact that he had had a conversation with Liz's mother explained everything.

"And?"

Patrick looked bemused. "Well she told me you were helping her."

Would he never get to the point? Hannah thought irritably. She could be back home with Elizabeth. She looked at her watch in an obvious manner. Patrick took the clue. "I'm sorry, I'm detaining you. Do you have another appointment to get to?" he asked rather formally.

Hannah relented and smiled. "Yes with my daughter's bathtime."

Patrick smiled too. "Ah yes. Baby Elizabeth. I have…"

"Look, I'm sorry Patrick that you have a problem but I'm not sure why you are telling me or in fact even wanted to see me. The police…"

"Have interviewed me several times about the murder. They know nothing about the blackmail and I have to keep it that way which is why I wanted to see you. Lady Rayman spoke so highly of you and, of course, I know you need to be paid but…"

"Hold on – need to be paid for what?" Patrick's last words had come out in a rush and Hannah was now completely confused.

"Well to help me of course. I need you to deal with the perpetrator."

Hannah was momentarily at a loss for words. Lady Rayman really shouldn't have given the impression to the priest that she was some sort of private investigator. Had he confided in Liz's mother?

"I'm sorry, I don't know what Lady Rayman has told you but I'm just a freelance journalist who…"

"Who is helping her make some enquiries about Liz's murder. "

"Ye-es but…"

"Supposing the two things are linked? The blackmail and murder? Looking into one might lead to clues about the other and I am prepared to pay you, Hannah. I need help and I need your complete discretion."

Hannah stared at the piece of paper she was holding. It was the second post mortem report that Lady Rayman had requested at was only natural, she supposed. Would she have asked Patrick, if he hadn't been indisposed?

"I'm sorry," she mumbled.

The bishop took her hands. "I am very sorry for your loss Hannah and for the terrible ordeal you have had. It must have been difficult for you so soon after…"

He left the sentence unfinished. Hannah felt a wave of fear wash over her as she looked up into his face. Behind his glasses, those eyes were stern, at variance with the sympathetic smile he affected. That hardness took her straight back to her confrontation with Gerald Lacon. The evil he perpetrated and what he had planned to do. She felt the bile rise. How did this bishop know? What did he know? Hannah had to speak to Tom even more urgently now.

"Thank you. Excuse me but Lady Rayman asked me to check on the caterers."

"Of course." But he wasn't going to let her off his hook so easily. "I understand you went to see Fr Patrick."

Hannah just stared at him, saying nothing.

"Don't meddle, Hannah, with matters which are no concern of yours."

The skin at the back of her neck was crawling with icy apprehension. She felt a tremour run through her as he followed her in, as though stalking her soul. She made a show of finding the caterer and having a few words. There was no need. Everything has been meticulously planned, the food laid out as if by a wave of a wand and glasses filled with wine were being circulated on trays by silent waiters. Hannah noticed Liz's "missionaries" – those who were probably the hungriest – hang back from the food. As though it were "family last". A few were lighting candles at a side table.

Hannah mingled, and was stopped and hugged by friends some of whom she hadn't seen for a long while. Suddenly there was James

Hannah's instigation after Tom had advised her. He was certainly right. There seemed to be a discrepancy between the Home Office Pathologist's findings and those of Dr Matthew Carter.

Dr Carter had found a needle mark on Liz's arm but there had been no suggestion of drugs, illegal or legal, in her blood samples. The slight bruising around the mark (how did the police PM miss this?) suggested that the needle may have been inserted against the victim's will.

Nausea threatened to overcome Hannah as the scene in Liz's make-shift surgery forced itself unpon her. The blood... Liz's slashed throat. Liz had suffered a heart attack but there was never anything to suggest she had a cardiac problem.

Maybe it was just the violence of the attack?

She wondered if she would gain more by actually speaking to Dr Carter. The needle mark certainly added a new dimension. Hannah sighed. She knew she was way out ofher depth. She dialled the pathologist's number and didn't know whether to be relieved or not when he answered himself.

"Ah yes, Lady Rayman said you might contact me," he said after Hannah had introduced herself.

"What do you think could have been injected, Dr Carter?"

"Well, for something that would leave no trace afterwards it could have been a massive dose of adrenaline which would have made her heart give out."

"But what about the slash to the neck?"

"That would have been done afterwards – presumably to make it look like an attack by one of her patients high on drink or drugs."

"To cover the real reason for her murder."

"That's a definite possibility. Do you have any theories?"

"None at all." Hannah sighed.

"In my experience, the reason is always there to be seen.

Sometimes you need to look at the problem from a different angle."

Hannah thanked Dr Carter and left him her number just in case he thought of anything else.

Why would anyone want to kill Liz? The police conclusion that it was a frenzied attack by a drink or drug-fuelled tramp seemed to be discredited now.

And what about Jacob Gurnstein? Why had he died – or committed suicide as far as the police were concerned? Hannah thought of DI Turner and her supercilious smile. Should she contact the patronising bitch?

Oh Tom why aren't you here? But she hadn't heard from Tom for a couple of days. Transatlantic calls were expensive but she could really do with hearing his voice right now. Sharing what she had discovered with him. He'd know exactly what to do.

As if on cue, the telephone rang. But if Hannah expected to hear Tom's voice she was sorely disappointed. It was the last person she wanted to speak to – Paul.

"Hi Hannah. I'm sorry we got off on such a bad footing yesterday but I really would like to meet up with you and discuss seeing my daughter on a regular basis."

"You shit! How dare you call her your daughter. All she has of you is half her genes. You are nothing to her and I intend to make sure it remains that way!"

There was the briefest of pauses before Paul said, "What on earth has got into you, Hannah? Does what we once had mean nothing to you?"

Hannah almost exploded. "You made it perfectly clear that it meant nothing to you when you asked me to have a termination and then walked away from the situation."

"I think you're being a little unfair, what I said was – "

"What you said was you did want children at some stage but didn't want to have one with me, if I remember correctly."

"Oh I didn't say that, did I? What I meant was…"

"Paul what on earth are you doing? Why have you decided this is the time to contact us?"

"Well I obviously heard about Liz and know how close you two were. I was worried. I thought you might welcome some support."

"I have support."

"So I heard." The words were quietly spoken but there was something in the tone that made the hairs on the back of her neck tingle.

"And what did you hear, Paul?"

"Oh just that you are friendly with a certain detective inspector who's been shipped off to the US following some sort of scandal last year involving the death of prostitutes who…" his voice petered out as he realised he had said too much.

"Now I wonder where you heard that fairy tale?" And what on earth led him to such a revelation? Hannah's voice was hard as steel. "I really don't think we have anything more to say."

She replaced the received with studied calm when inside she was volcanic. She felt hot then cold then hot again. Her hands were shaking and she felt near to collapse. How did he know? And, more to the point how much did he know? The prostitutes' deaths were common knowledge. She concetrated on getting her breathing under control. But he had mentioned a scandal and that was the very thing that had been hushed up. Her story had been spiked. The cover up had been forensically achieved. So what did Paul know and what was he involved in to have discovered it?

That, Hannah decided, she'd make it her business to find out.

ELEVEN

"If you commit one very bad sin, a monstrous sin, does it wipe out all the good you have done or tried to achieve in your life?" Those words came back to her as she dialled the number for St John's vicarage.

Father Patrick had stared into her eyes. She recalled her embarrassment – she was certainly way out of her comfort zone.

"That wasn't a rhetorical question…"

"Surely you are in a far better position to answer that, than I am?"

Hannah remembered the priest's anguished look as he had opened the taxi door for her after she had agreed to help him. "Thank you." He smiled but sadness was etched deeply into his features.

"Hello this is St John's Vicarage. Father Patrick is unable to take your call but please leave a message and…"

Hannah hung up. That was the third time she'd called. She'd left a message the first time, just asking the priest to call her but that was four hours ago and she thought he'd have checked his messages by now. It gave her an uneasy feeling. She looked at the leaflet he'd given her detailing all the church services. None was scheduled for this morning but there were evening prayers at five o'clock. Maybe she should just turn up?

Hannah could hear the murmur of voices and headed towards them. Two rather smartly dressed women sat conspicuously apart from three people who, from their attire, looked as though they were from Cardboard City. Just to one side the priest sat reading the prayers and pausing as the tiny congregation made the responses. As Hannah approached the priest looked up and smiled. She stood rooted to the spot. It was not Father Patrick.

The priest waved his hand to a seat and continued. Hannah sat down and one of the tramps indicated the page they were on in the prayer book. Hannah's mouth was so dry she could only mouth the unfamiliar words. In contrast her hands were clammy and her heart was pounding. At last the service seemed to be coming to a conclusion as the priest said: "May Christ, who has opened the kingdom of heaven, bring us to reign with him in glory."

There was a mumbled "Amen".

"Let us bless the Lord. Alleluia, alleluia."

This time the response was a little louder: "Thanks be to God. Alleluia, alleluia."

For a few moments there was silence then everyone started making moves to leave.

"Hello – are you all right? You looked as though you'd seen a ghost when you came in." The priest had sat down beside her, his white cropped hair in sharp contrast to his black clerical robes. "Is there anything I can help you with. I…"

"Where's Father Patrick?" Even to her own ears she sounded rude. "I'm sorry, it's just I came here specifically to see him. Is he at the vicarage?"

Something changed in the priest's expression. Briefly he looked angry but this was quickly replaced with a smile.

"I'm sorry he's been called away."

"Where?"

"I'm afraid I'm not at liberty to say but he could be gone for some time. Is there anything I can help you with?"

"I'm not sure… There was a murder here not long ago… My friend Liz Rayman –

"Aye the dentist lady," one of the tramps who had been standing nearby interrupted. "Terrible. Terrible thing." He looked close to tears and sat down abruptly.

Hannah thought the priest looked irritated. She was right.

"Well I don't want to rush you but I have to get over to St Faith's for Mass. Perhaps we could continue this conversation…?"

The invitation hung in the air.

"Can I contact Fr Patrick by letter?

"You could try sending a letter care of the Archdeacon but I wouldn't count on receiving a reply in the near future."

"But I don't understand…"

The priest looked distincly uncomfortable. "Give me your telephone number and I'll see what I can do."

Hannah fished in her bag then handed him her card. "And you are?"

"Father Anthony. And now I really must lock up the church and leave."

Hannah heard her name. It came again. "Hannah…"

"Yes?" she listened for a reply. Nothing. The room was completely dark and she realised that she must have been dreaming. She turned to look at the clock radio. 3.45. That's all she needed – another broken night's sleep. But these days, it wasn't Elizabeth who disturbed her slumbers but her namesake Liz. Elizabeth now slept through the night. Liz would sleep forever.

She could feel the sob rise in her throat. During the day it was easier to guard against the horrendous thoughts that threatened to overcome her at night. She wondered how Lady Rayman coped. How do you carry on living when your child has not just died but been brutally murdered? Senselessly killed it would seem. There was no rhyme or reason as to why anyone would want to end to a life that not only had done much good, going out to work in areas of desperate need but which also had had the promise of another life. A double tragedy. Her last image of Liz seemed seered onto her eyelids every time she closed her eyes. She was way out of her depth, just as Tom had suggested.

Hannah's thoughts anchored on Tom. She hadn't heard from him since their brief conversation after Celia had had the private post mortem carried out. She wondered why. None of the police who were purportedly investigating Liz's murder had been in contact with her or returned her calls. A conspiracy of silence culminating in Father Patrick's disappearance. No one had contacted her from whomever it was in the church who dealt with these matters. Although what matters these were Hannah was at a loss to know.

Hannah picked up the notebook she kept on her bedside table. If she couldn't sleep, she could make a list of things she needed to do. But pencil poised, she wrote nothing. Something was eluding her, she knew. And above all else she knew that Liz's funeral was being planned by her mother who had asked Hannah to read a poem and say a few words. With terrible clarity she remembered the last funeral when she'd delivered the eulogy. Caroline's. No comparison.

She thought of those who had attended – prostitutes, tramps who turned out to be not what they seemed. The sad lost property clerk. What was his name? It saddened Hannah that she no longer remembered. But maybe there was someone just like him at Waterloo?

She thought of the men and women living rough in what was termed "Cardboard City" in the underpasses by the station and opposite the church. Maybe she should make an effort to engage with them.

The thought didn't appeal. Some of them looked terrifying and for the life of her she couldn't understand how Liz had come to be working with them. At least for Father Patrick it must have been part of his mission.

Remembering their conversation and his assertion he was being backmailed, Hannah wondered if there was any connection to his disappearance and Liz's death. She had no idea how the church hierarchy worked but assumed he had been whisked away from harm.

Then a thought that had been niggling at the periphery of her mind crept into her consciousness. She didn't know how the church worked but she knew a man who did. Reverend John Daniels, the priest who had agreed to offer Caroline a safe refuge in Essex. Maybe he could shed some light on what might be going on.

She made a note to phone him later and switched off the lamp hoping sleep would claim her for a couple of hours. But as soon as she closed her eyes she was back in Liz's makeshift consulting room in St John's. Exhausted and hovering between sleep and wakefulness she saw Liz mouthing something to her. But no sound emerged. Hannah called out to her, her face wet with tears.

"You haven't spoken much about your time in Somalia?" Hannah poured some more wine into their glasses. They had finished the meal but were still sitting at the dining table.

Liz smiled but her eyes looked immeasurably sad. "Oh you know, I don't want to become a charity bore." She stared into her glass. "When you see how people are living there, it makes me feel so humble but also frustrated and…" she took a sip of wine. "Did you know that there is almost 100 per cent female genital mutilation there? We had no impact on reducing that. Girls have no rights. They're the ones who walk miles each day to fetch water for the family. Every time they go outside to the loo they risk being raped or assaulted. If they are lucky enough to go to school, once they menstruate they miss a quarter of their education. You can't begin to imagine…"

Hannah had been thinking of her own daughter as Liz spoke. They were so fortunate yet there were inequalities in the west as well. Her eyes misted as she thought of Caroline and what she had been through.

Liz put her hand over Hannah's. "Sorry I didn't mean to upset you. It's so difficult now that I'm back to find any perspective. And there were some strange people working there."

"What do you mean, strange?"

Liz took a gulp of wine. "I don't know really. Misfits I suppose. Not drop-outs exactly but people who have had problems in their own society. Not all of them obviously – there were some really great philanthropists working there but sometimes I did wonder about the motives of some of them."

"And where did you fit in? High-minded philanthropist?" Hannah smiled to reduce the implied criticsm of her words. She still hurt from what she saw as Liz's desertion when she was pregnant and now she was back she seemed distant. She felt Liz's attitude towards her was judgemental.

Liz ignored the jibe. "So how's motherhood treating you then?"

"Good. I love it. But sometimes I feel a bit overwhelmed by it all."

"Well it was your choice…"

"I know." Hannah wondered at Liz's tone. They were both scratchy with each other. Probably because they hadn't seen each other for so long. There were experiences both had had that distanced them from each other. She hadn't meant she was overwhelmed in a negative sense but in a positive one. Overwhelmed by love. She found Elizabeth endlessly fascinating. Always adorable. But to say all that might have seemed to be gloating, boasting. And Liz seemed immensely sensitive to mentions of babies and children at the moment.

"Anyway I'd better make a move – I'm doing my first clinic at St John's tomorrow. Just wonder if anyone will turn up."

"How on earth were you persuaded to take that on?"

"I imagine in a similar way that you were persuaded to take in a beaten up prostitute – because I care. I might be a 'high minded philanthropist' but at least I can put my skills to practical use."

"Meaning I can't?"

"Good lord, no Hannah. What you tried to do was admirable. In fact you did manage to get that place closed down and the ringleader deported. Just because your story wasn't published doesn't mean it didn't have repercussions. A real and lasting impact."

Liz phoned for a cab. "It was lovely to catch up and thanks for dinner. My treat next time."

A toot from outside announced the cab's arrival. They hugged in the hallway and Hannah watched her get into the car before closing and locking the door.

There was some wine left in the bottle that she poured into her glass and sat down to watch Newsnight. But she wasn't really paying attention to the discussion between political pundits.

She felt saddened that her friendship with Liz was so strained. Perhaps because there was so much they couldn't tell or explain to each other. Hannah's thoughts strayed to Tom. She missed him but they'd never had a chance to grow into what she would have called a proper relationship. Almost soon as they were free to see each other, Tom accepted the placement in New York. He said he had to play the game whatever that meant. But why? Was she still at risk?

After the appalling scene with Gerald Lacon in her own home, Hannah had thought about moving away. But what good would that serve? Problems didn't disappear with a change of address. But she didn't want to live her life continually looking over her shoulder. Always worrying? What effect would that have on Elizabeth?

The wine mellowed her thoughts…

She woke up stiff and cold. The heating had gone off. The television was a blank screen. "Shit," she thought and decided to leave all the dinner things and just go to bed.

In the bathroom she studied her face in the mirror. Her mascara had smudged accentuating the dark circles under her eyes. She looked the wreck she felt herself to be as she cleansed and moisturised her face and neck and then cleaned her teeth, wishing, as she spat out the toothpaste, she could clear her life of evil just as easily.

She didn't turn the light on in her room. Another precaution she'd got used to. Before closing the curtains, she stared out of the window. The bedroom light at number nine across the road was on. As always. The dark outline of a fox stalked silently down the centre of the road. Everything else was still. Silent but for the faraway sounds now and again of car doors opening and closing. Nothing to worry herself about but there was always that niggling fear.

She drew the curtains, stripped off and slipped into bed. Hopefully Elizabeth wouldn't wake too early. The new nanny, Janet, was a capable young woman and Hannah felt she could trust her. Well she wouldn't have employed her if she hadn't and Tom had helped with ways to check out her background and references. In the half-awake moment before sleep claimed her she saw Caroline's face. Smiling at her. At peace now, she hoped, although she herself had no belief in an afterlife it was reassuring to think of souls or whatever essence remained of someone in life found rest and were never disturbed again.

Amen she thought. So be it.

TWELVE

The train from Liverpool Street was on time and Hannah had only just made it into the carriage as the whistle blew. Perhaps bringing Elizabeth with her had been a mistake as manoeuvring the buggy had slowed her down. Now she sat down heavily and drew her breath. Elizabeth had nodded off but not so the only other occupant who took out a cigarette and lit up.

Hannah coughed. "Excuse me, this is a no smoking compartment."

If she'd expected an apology and a swift extinction of the offending cigarette she was sadly deceived.

"So?" The young man looked at her with such beligerance that Hannah metaphorically shrank.

"So you shouldn't be smoking and I have a child with me."

"If you don't like it move." He put his feet up on the opposite seat, crossing his ankles, then exhaled smoke in her direction. She got up and moved the buggy as far away as possible. She could feel her face flushing and she was perilously close to tears.

As she sat down again, her mobile phone rang.

"Hannah Weybridge." The youth looked over to her and she wondered at his look of interest at her name. "What can I do for you Detective Inspector Turner?" She hoped that the mention of a police officer would warn the young man off. But as she listened to the precise tones of Claudia Turner telling her that Father Patrick Ryan was in intensive care at St Thomas's and that the reason she had contacted Hannah was that he had her card on him when he was found.

"Found?"

"Yes he was found wandering along Waterloo Bridge, clearly in extreme distress. Look I don't want to discuss this over the phone. Where are you?"

"On a train to Essex. I'll be back early evening."

"Right could you let me know when you're home and I'll come over." She cut the line not waiting for Hannah's reply.

No if that's all right with you, thought Hannah. Then thought how uncharitable that was. At least she'd let her know about Patrick. She wondered if her journey to see Reverend John Daniels was now superfluous.

The man in question was at the station to meet them. She'd interviewed John Daniels a couple of years ago about a street project he was involved in and that was what had given her the idea of despatching Caroline to him for safety. Sadly that had never happened. She hadn't been able to protect her and had ended up putting her own daughter's life at risk.

"Hannah – lovely to see you and you must be Elizabeth." He had squatted down to be at face height with the toddler who was all giggles and smiles after her nap.

"Come on the car's over here and I have a child seat in the back." He led the way to a rather smart looking pale blue car. It seemed an incongruous vehicle for a small town priest.

The vicar must have read her thoughts. "My one indulgence… and I need a car that I can rely on not to break down when I'm on call."

Hannah nodded although she wasn't sure what he meant. The warmth inside and the movement of the car was having a soporific effect.

"Here we are." The Reverend John Daniels's voice broke into her dream-like state and she realised they had arrived at the vicarage, situated next door to St Mark's, an imposing Norman church with its squat square tower and two stained glass windows she could see from the road.

The priest opened a side door and shouted, "Hello we're here" as they entered. Hannah wondered if that announcement was a gentle warning? She had no idea who lived here.

"Welcome Hannah. I'm Alice, John's wife." A tall slim woman with long blonde hair held back in a scrunchie and wearing what looked like woollen leggings and a thick hand-knitted jumper, clasped her hand. "And you must be Elizabeth," she said to the wide-eyed toddler. "Come in, come in."

They went straight into a large oak beamed kitchen with exposed brickwork and free standing cupboards some of which looked on the brink of keeling over under the weight of shelves of mismatched crockery and an ecclectic range of souvenirs. Hannah smiled and thought of the contrast to Liz's minimalist appartment. It pulled her up short as she had thought of her friend in joy rather than the bleak sadness that usually invaded her consciousness.

"Tea? Coffee?" John – as he had asked Hannah to call him – waved a kettle at her.

"Coffee please and could I warm this up for Elizabeth?" Hannah produced a meal she'd prepared.

"Of course." Alice took the plastic container and popped it into a microwave. When it was ready she handed it to Hannah who fed Elizabeth with her sitting on her lap. The child managed to get more over her face than in her mouth as her gaze went from Alice to John, then back to her mother.

"How was your journey," Alice asked.

"Fine except for some yob smoking in the compartment."

Alice tutted in commiseration as she opened the fridge and produced a huge platter of sandwiches. "Didn't know what you'd like so I made a selection." She placed them on the large wooden table that dominated the kitchen, together with some plates and a bowl of fruit.

"Shall I take Elizabeth with me and leave you two to talk in peace?" She held out her hand to the toddler who with little encouragement grasped her fingers and waddled off.

Alice's smile seemed to linger after she had gone like the Cheshire cat.

John gave Elizabeth a little wave goodbye then his expression became more serious. "Before anything else Hannah, I want to say how sorry I was to hear about Caroline. Her death and and the repercussions must have been profoundly disturbing for you. You have been in my prayers –" he waved a hand as if to dismiss whatever she was about to say – "prayers still work for the unbelievers or the unconvinced," he said and poured their coffees.

"Thank you," she said as much for the coffee as the spiritual intervention on her behalf.

"And of course I am praying for the soul of your dear friend. Such a terrible thing and to have witnessed..." he bit into a sandwich and left the sentence unfinished.

"I met the vicar from St John's afterwards. He ... well he told me he was being blackmailed and that it could be linked to Liz's death." John's gaze did not leave her face and his expression didn't change. To her surprise he didn't seem shocked or disbelieving.

"I'm not sure about how all this fits together because when I tried to ring him I got the answerphone all the time. So I went to evening prayers and there was another priest there who said that Father Patrick had gone away and would be so for the foreseeable…"

"Hm sounds like some sort of disciplinary…"

"Yes perhaps, but on the way here I had a call from the police inspector investigating Liz's murder saying that he'd been found wandering on Waterloo Bridge in extreme distress."

John stirred two spoonfuls of sugar into his coffee. "Curiouser and curiouser. I assume he's in hospital then?" Hannah nodded. "He should be safe there. Who was the priest you saw at St John's?"

"A Father Andrew – he didn't give me a surname but I gave him my card. I don't really know anything about Father Patrick – he'd found out about me from Lady Rayman. He wanted to employ me, can you believe it?"

"Why not. If you hadn't been stopped you'd have exposed a particularly sinister group in London last year." He sipped his coffee.

"You read Caroline's diaries."

"I did." He waited to see how Hannah reacted but she just shrugged.

"I'm glad. It means someone else knows…"

"Yes and I have the copy safely stored away in case we ever need to use it. Now, back to Patrick. He asked for your help."

"Yes but what on earth can I do?"

"Well, to start with you must have more confidence in yourself, Hannah. Lady Rayman obviously rates you and I don't suppose she knows one iota of what happened with that outfit last year."

The country parish priest went on to give Hannah a lesson in how dioceses are run and who was who. By the time he took them back to the railway station, Hannah felt a little less in the dark and also buoyed by the reassurance that John Daniels would help her in any way he could when she needed him.

THIRTEEN

Claudia Turner arrived half an hour after Elizabeth had finally given up the struggle to stay awake. Hannah had just about managed to tidy a few things away and would have liked to have had the time to shower and change after all that travelling.

The DI looked immaculate which irritated Hannah even more. But she was completely thrown when Claudia waved a bottle of white wine in front of her. "Sorry to intrude on your evening –" she looked anything but sorry – "but this is chilled…"

"Thanks." Hannah stood aside for her to enter and followed her into the sitting room.

Claudia sat on one of the sofas and relaxed back into the cushions. A totally different person from the first time they'd met. "God it's been a long day."

"Sorry I'll get some glasses." She felt wrong-footed and surprised especially when she returned and saw that Claudia had picked up one of Elizabeth's books and was leafing through it.

She smiled as Hannah handed her a glass of wine. "I need this." Correctly interpreting Hannah's expression, she continued, "It's ok, I'm not driving. My DC is waiting in the car. Thought it would be easier to talk on our own." She took a deep slug of wine.

Hannah sat down opposite her. "You said on the phone that Fr Patrick Ryan had been found wandering on Waterloo Bridge?"

"Yes, well thereabouts. One of the tramps who inhabit Cardboard City saw him and managed to get him to St Thomas's. No mean feat I would have thought. The priest was all over the place and had trouble walking in a straight line." She drank some more wine. "What's your connection with him?"

Hannah sipped her wine wondering how candid she should be. "I'm not sure I have one really. He asked me to visit the church after Liz… after I had found Liz there. He was the one who'd asked her to set up the drop-in …"

"And you gave him your card?"

"No, strangely I don't remember giving him a card. When he rang me I assumed he'd got my number from Lady Rayman."

"Well he had it in his pocket when he was admitted to hospital. Uniform made the connection and informed me. When did you last see him?"

"A few days ago. I tried ringing him but just got the answerphone so I went back to St John's hoping to catch him there." Hannah went quiet and sipped some wine.

"And?" Claudia had finished her wine and she got up, refilled her glass and topped up Hannah's.

"Thank you. He wasn't there. There was another priest who told me Fr Patrick had gone away and couldn't be contacted. Or rather he said I could send a letter for him to the archdeacon and it might get passed on."

"And did you?" Hannah looked up blankly. None of this made sense. If Patrick had been whisked away how was that he was found wandering on Waterloo Bridge? "Did you write to him?" Claudia prompted.

"No. I hadn't really known what to say. I knew he was devastated by Liz's murder but then so am I…" she blinked rapidly hoping to disperse the tears which threatened. "Is he still in hospital?"

"Yes he's in intensive care – he was drugged up to the eyeballs?

"Drugged?"

Claudia Turner was watching her carefully. A glass or two of wine didn't dull her antennae. She was intrigued by this woman and her connections with this case. She had considered contacting Tom Jordan then thought better of it.

"I don't for one minute think he was a user. Someone had adminsitered a large quantity of heroin; he was raving." What the DI omitted to tell the journalist was that he bore all the signs of having been systematically beaten as well. It looked as though he had been interrogated. "Presumably the person or persons responsible wanted him out of the way for some reason. Any thoughts on that, Hannah?"

"Good lord, no. Do you think it might have been self-administered? He seemed very upset when I met him. Maybe he was too distraught to think clearly – or wanted to stop thinking?"

"Interesting theory. Anyway we'll know more when he's detoxed, I suppose."

"Can I visit him?"

"I'd hoped you'd say that," Claudia smiled. Hannah found this friendly side to the inspector more disconcerting that the former haughty, hostile one. "He's in a private room and has police protection. We're not taking any chances after Jacob Gurnstein's death …"

"So you don't think he killed Liz and committed suicide then?"

"Let's just say I don't think he killed himself. And the priest turning up like that just adds more complications." Claudia finished her wine and place the glass on the table. "The bishop's jumping up and down about access as well but until Fr Patrick is able to tell us what's happened they'll be kept away."

"Is that legal?"

Claudia's arched eyebrow was more eloquent that her "Probably not but for the time being that's the line we're sticking to."

"Right. So when can I visit?"

"Two tomorrow afternoon? Whoever's on duty will be told to expect you." She smiled again. "We'll see what a friendly face can achieve." She stood up to leave. "Have you heard from Tom recently?"

Hannah was surprised by the question but steeled herself not to show any reaction which might betray her. "He phoned a few days ago. Why?"

"No reason. Just thought you could do with some moral support, that's all. Give him my love."

At the door, she paused. "Take care, Hannah," she said quietly and touched her lightly on the arm.

"Is this an official conversation?" Tom Jordan's voice was calm and Claudia Turner could almost hear his smile. She had revised her decision not to call him.

"Yes and no. I just wanted to check what you know about Hannah Weybridge's involvement with St John's apart from the obvious fact that her best friend was killed there."

"As far as I know there isn't any. I don't think she attends church at all …"

"I don't mean that. She seems to have struck up some sort of relationship with the vicar."

"Has she?" Tom sounded surprised.

"Well he had her card on him when he was admitted to hospital after a massive heroin overdose."

"What?" Tom sounded genuinely astonished.

Good. Maybe that would prompt him to contact Hannah. "It's complicated Tom. But I'm worried that Hannah know more than she's telling. That could be dangerous."

Tom muttered something she couldn't make out. Clearly he wasn't giving anything away either.

"How's it going on your side of the pond?"

Tom was vague and managed to terminate the conversation on his terms.

Well, well, Claudia Turner thought. Maybe he wasn't as impervious as he seemed. She was concerned for Hannah although she couldn't pinpoint why. She wasn't the stereotypical door-steppping hack. She liked her. In other circumstances they might have been friends.

Hannah had made herself a sandwich – she seemed to live off them these days – and poured the rest of the wine into her glass. She felt empty and alone. Nothing made sense. Liz murderd, Jacob Gurnstein fished out of the Thames and now Fr Patrick given a massive heroin overdose. She presumed he was supposed to have died as well and wondered who had had the wherewithal to get him to hospital and save his life.

It was all senseless and as if that wasn't enough Paul had steamed back into her life as well. What was his game? And how did she know about Caroline? She felt scared. And to top it all she had an editorial meeting at *The News* in the morning. That was something she could definitely do without.

FOURTEEN

"So Hannah, any progress on the Liz Rayman murder story?"

The editorial meeting had dragged on for an hour. Georgina Henderson, the editor, loved the sound of her own voice. She seemed to delight in overturning any decisions her deputy, Terry Cornhill, had made in her absence. Hannah squirmed in her chair as she caught the gleam of pure malice directed at her from Judy Burton.

"No not really – I had to hand over anything I've found to the police. Jacob Gurnstein, one of her Cardboard City patients, was found drowned in the Thames. Police think he may have been the perpetrator …" Some instinct made Hannah hold back on what DI Turner had told her and about Fr Patrick. Self preservation?

"Right we'll just let the crime desk take over the story." Hannah was about to protest then held her tongue as she continued, "Hannah I liked the piece you wrote on what it was like to discover a close friend brutally murdered –" she paused as if for dramatic effect, taking in Judy's furious expression – "so I'd like you to continue liaising with Rory. Work with him on any leads that come your way. You could also write a short piece on the funeral. We'll send along a photographer as will most of the other nationals but with you we'll have the march on them."

"Let's hope you can manage that," Judy murmered just loud enough for everyone to hear.

"I don't think so." Hannah, face aflame picked up her notebook and bag and stood to leave.

"May I remind you Hannah, you are on a retainer. You do have a contract with us." Ms Henderson looked like a bored headmistress remonstrating with a stroppy student. "Minimum one thousand words in time for the late edition. And a few personal pixs showing the two of you together would help the piece as well."

"I'm sure you can manage that, at least." Judy Burton was enjoying Hannah's predicament. "I'd be happy to help with any rewrites."

I bet you would, thought Hannah.

The meeting was winding up when Richard, the sports editor and one-time lover of Judy Burton, said in a stage whisper, "So how's it going with Paul. Is he Mr Right in the long line of possible Mr Rights?"

Judy flushed. "Shut up Richard. What would you know about being Mr Right? Or even Mr Might Have Been Right if he'd made an effort?"

There were a few smirks and mumbles among the others. "Okay boys and girls off you go." The editor's dismissal brooked no argument.

Outside the office door, Rory touched her arm. "Don't take all this so personally. Just write a really good piece for me – and make sure I get it in time to read through and offer any suggestions before the rabble."

"Thanks Rory." Hannah really did appreciate his help and suport. "So who's the new love interest then? Anyone we know?"

"No someone who works in the city. Has his own company or something. Paul … Monty-something or other…"

"Paul Montague?" Hannah could feel her grasp on reality slipping. Her arms felt leaden. Her pulse was throbbing in her neck and she wondered if her legs could support her any longer.

"Yeah something like that – Hannah are you ok? You look like you've seen the proverbial… Sit down. Now."

Rory pushed her on to a nearby chair. For a moment the whole world was black. She could feel Rory pressing a cup of water to her lips. "Drink," he commanded. She sipped until the colours returned.

"Christ you gave me quite a turn then. What happened?"

They were sitting in the pub across the road from the offices. It was too early for the lunchtime crowd so they'd found a table in the corner and Rory had bought her a brandy and a sandwich.

"Thank you." She was touched by his kindness. And very grateful. If she'd actually fainted to the floor in the office she could imagine the ensuing scene. Rory had saved her and preserved what little dignity she had.

"Well? Can't you tell Uncle Rory?" He smiled and the crinkles at the corner of his eyes made him look so kind so… so easy to confide in … but Hannah held back. She never knew who she could trust these days. And this wasn't the right moment for confidences.

"Oh I didn't have time to eat anything for breakfast this morning…"

"And the name… Paul Montague?" Rory wasn't stupid and he certainly wouldn't appreciate being played for a fool.

"I once knew a Paul Montague that's all. Probably not the same guy."

"No probably not – eat your sandwich." Rory, she could see, was not convinced.

FIFTEEN

As she walked along its corridors, Hannah wondered how often Fr Patrick had had to visit St Thomas's Hospital to comfort his sick or bereaved parishoners. The hospital was large and seemed impersonal but Patrick was probably well known – and, it would seem well loved – here among the staff. So far there had been no leaks to the press and Hannah imagined the powers that be at the diocese would be working like mad at damage limitation. But there was always someone who was after a quick buck.

It made her wonder about the homeless person who had brought him in. He could have made some money with his story. Unless someone had paid him off. Silenced him with cash.

Hannah took the lift to the 12th floor and having checked in at the nurses' station followed their directions to the private rooms. She knew which one was Patrick's by the police constable stationed at the door.

"Do you have some ID, Ms Weybridge?" he asked when she told him who she was.

She was prepared for this and as a non-driver had remembered to tuck her passport into her bag just before leaving home. She felt reassured that they were obviously taking this latest incident seriously but wondered why Claudia Turner had included her in the people who know, when she knew she was under condtract to *The News*. Maybe Tom had had a word with her? That possibility seemed unlikely given his obvious antipathy to her getting involved in any way.

"Thanks." The police officer handed back her passport and opened the door for her.

The room was silent but for intermittent bleeps from a machine by the side of the bed. It felt utterly peaceful as though God's own angels had descended to protect one of their own. What a fanciful thought! Hannah was surprised by it. Then she looked at the bed where lay the priest.

From what she could see above the sheet that covered most of him, he was wearing a hospital gown. There was stubble on his face and his hair looked dirty. Drips were attached to his body, presumably part of the detoxing process, his eyes were firmly closed and his breathing sounded laboured from under the oxygen mask.

A nurse entered the room. "Sorry, just have to do a few obs."

"Shall I wait outside?"

"No, you're okay." She lifted Patrick's limp wrist and checked her watch as she look his pulse and made a note of it. "Are you a relative? The police are being very careful about who comes in here."

"No, I'm –" what was she? "I'm a friend." Even friend seemed to overstate her relationship.

"Well sit yourself down and talk to him. He's still very poorly but he will hear you."

After taking and recording his temperature and checkng the drips, she bustled out closing the door gently behind her.

Hannah did as she was told and sat beside the bed. Gingerly she placed her hand over Patrick's. It felt cool and unresponsive.

"Patrick, I don't know whether you can hear me. It's Hannah. Hannah Weybridge. Liz Rayman's friend. We met last week." She thought there was a slight movement in his hand when she mentioned Liz's name but had probably imagined it.

"Oh Patrick – who did this to you? Why?" How pathetic, she thought, I'm trying to question an unconscious man!

Instead she switched to telling him about her relationship with Liz. "I was really surprised when she said she was setting up a drop-in clinic in your church. Although I shouldn't have been, given the way she went off and served with that health charity in Somalia. She was a good soul although I never knew she had any interest in the church. Perhaps she didn't. But how did you persuade her?" By now Hannah was just thinking out loud. "I wonder what Claudia Turner thought I could achieve by coming here? I thought you'd be conscious. Well at least you didn't die. Did you know that Liz was pregnant? I didn't but I think she was going to tell me that evening, that evening when..."

The tears were streaming down her face, and she was back in the room with one of her closest friends. Her dead friend. She sniffed loudly trying to control her sobs when a tissue found its way into her hand and she blew her nose loudly. Looking up she was stunned to see Claudia Turner immaculate as ever standing by her with a packet of tissues.

"Sorry I…"

"No need to apologise. It was a long shot…"

"But you knew he wasn't conscious… so why all this, this… this –" Hannah couldn't think of an appropriate word.

"As I said, a long shot…"

"Is there anything I can do for him?"

"Be a friend. I think he'll need one."

"Well, surely he …"

"Hannah all I can tell you is this – we've started digging up the garden at the back of the vicarage. It will be on the six o'clock news. The Bishop is apoplectic. They may now get in touch with you as you gave your card to that priest at St John's. Try to say as little as possible about what you know."

"I don't know anything …"

"It may be more than you think. Just tread carefully. Be wary – with everyone."

"Even you?" Hannah tried a touch of humour that she was far from feeling.

"Especially me." But Claudia Turner was smiling. "I'll get a squad car to take you home."

"Please don't worry – I'll take the bus. Give myself time to think and stop the neighbours' tongues wagging."

"Yes I imagine you've had more than enough of that."

Their eyes met. Neither woman was giving much away. But one of them certainly knew more of the other and was not letting on.

Hannah touched Patrick's hand, then leaned over and kissed him lightly on the forehead. "Be safe Patrick, be safe."

They left the hospital together. "Sure I can't get you a lift?"

"No, I'll be fine, honestly."

"Well, take care." Claudia shook her hand. "Ring me if you hear anything or need to talk."

Hannah nodded and made her way to Westminster Bridge. But she wasn't going home. There were things she had to check out for herself.

At the bus stop she made herself wait for a Number 12 to Dulwich. She had no idea if anyone was watching her but if they were she had to look as though she were going home. Ten minutes later she had boarded the Routemaster but stayed near the open exit. At the next stop she got off and made her way into Waterloo station, leaving at the Waterloo Road exit. She took off the bright red scarf and wooly hat hoping that would make her less obvious. She fingered the loose change she'd put ready in her pocket and taking a deep breath descended into the underpass known as both the Bull Ring and Cardboard City.

The temperature seemed to have dropped a few degrees and the smell of urine, stale cigarette smoke, alcohol fumes, and vomit tested her resolve. The concrete walls and pavement underfoot reflected a sombre light from the few bulbs which were still working. What she initially took for piles of cardboard were actually makeshift homes. Some more elaborate than others. There seemed to be a pecking order in the constructions. Established "squatters" versus the incomers. Most were sitting beside their homes, many with eyes closed maybe willing themselves into another place. One rocked to and fro in jerky motion, another sat in still and silent meditation.

Hannah could only get a few shots from the hidden camera Rory had lent her from *The News* stash. If she walked any slower she really would draw the attention she needed to avoid.

"Oi luv, ain't you the woman who found our Lizzie?

Hannah turned to face a woman of indeterminate age, thining hair was grey in parts and chestnut in others, pulled back into a pony tail. Her clothes, everything about her, were nondescript, grey, the dirt so ingrained in the lines of her face it looked like stage make-up for some awful tragedy.

"I'm sorry?"

Hannah managed a few more shots and dropped some coins in the hat of a youngish man playing a recorder. Click.

"Leave 'er alone, Eileen. If you are the one who found Liz – I'm very sorry for your loss – and ours," he said as though an afterthought. Click. There was something about the man who had just spoken that was nudging a distant memory. Then she remembered he had been one of the tramps at St John's when she'd gone to find Patrick Ryan.

"Thank you." Hannah swallowed hard. "It must be very hard for you too. She was a very special lady.

"She was." The man grabbed her hand and as he stared into her face he pushed something between her fingers. "But don't let us keep you." She felt a little push and was walking away more quickly than she'd anticipated.

It was the time of day when light was transmuting into darkness. Winter afternoons. The sun's fading rays mocked her as she emerged from the underpass. They held no warmth and little illumination. She shuddered as she slipped the ball of paper that had been pushed into her hand into her bag, determined not to look at it until she could be sure she wasn't observed. This strategy had become second nature to her now. She should have been able to relax her guard. Tom had assured her she was safe. But was he just saying that to allay her fears? And why hadn't he called her?

By now she was outside St John's, stopping abruptly at the police tape which cut off the entrance. There seemed to be a lot of activity going on inside. Why hadn't Claudia mentioned this? She approached the constable who was standing to one side.

"Excuse me, but what's going on here?" she asked using the opportunity to take more photos.

"Part of an ongoing enquiry, miss."

Hannah flashed her press card but it got her no further information. She moved away and bumped straight into a black clad figure standing at the edge of the tape on the other side of the gateway. Father Anthony.

"Oh sorry – it's Father Anthony, isn't it?"

For a moment his steely grey eyes registered no recognition. Then he seemed to mentally pull himself together. In his job it didn't do to forget people.

"Forgive me. I was distracted by all this terrible, terrible desecration…

"Surely it's not as bad as …"

"Probably worse." He let out a long breath which might have been a sigh. "What can I do for you, Miss…"

"Weybridge, Hannah Weybridge. We met during a service when I'd come hoping to see Fr Patrick…" she reminded him.

"Yes, so you did." He paused staring into the dark interior of the church porchway which revealed nothing. "I am sorry for the loss of your friend. I fear I didn't show enough compassion the last time we met."

Hannah wanted to hit him! Did he graduate and measure how much compassion he should show for each type of loss, tragedy, grief? So much for pastoral empathy. Was his faith so shallow?

"We're all human," he said as though reading her thoughts, "even priests. Especially priests."

"Yes, well I wouldn't know." Hannah made an effort to calm her inner rage. "So do you know why they are in the church again? Is it anything to do with Liz Rayman's murder?"

"I shouldn't think so. Unless they've had new information. I think this is more to do with your erstwhile friend, Father Patrick."

"Why? What on earth could he have done?"

Father Anthony gave her a searching look. "What indeed. Excuse me I am needed."

Hannah had seen the taxi draw up. A rather short man in a

heavy overcoat with a scarf left open to reveal a clerical collar above a purple shirt, had emerged and stood with his head bowed before making his way to the police tape. Hannah managed a few shots before Fr Anthony blocked him from her sight.

There was nothing to be had from hanging around so she made her way down the side road to Roupell Street where the "vicarage" nestled between other houses. Indistinghuishable except it was now cordoned off.

"Well, well, well if it isn't Miss Weybridge." It was the voice of the unpleasant detective sergeant who had questioned her when she had found Liz's body. "And what may I ask are you doing here?"

Hannah parried with a question. "What do you mean, what am I doing here?"

"Seems a bit of a coincidenne, that's all. You turning up just as we're digging up the vicarage garden…" he licked his lips.

Hannah forced herself to smile. "Don't tell me you don't believe in coincidences, Sergeant." She glanced over at the open door and managed to take a few shots before she turned back. "If you must know I'm walking along this street making my way to the *Stamford Arms* where I'm meeting some friends for a drink. If that's any business of yours?"

"Convenient that your route takes you past Patrick Ryan's house…"

"I know all the back streets. Worked here for years."

"Really." The DS licked his upper lip and leered at her.

Hannah flushed. "I was employed at IPC." And the *Stamford Arms* was where they all drank so with a little luck on her side, someone would be in there who she knew well enough to greet to authenticate this fiction.

"Oh yes, I'd forgotten. Journalist, aren't you? Don't let us keep you then." The supercilious smile sickened her.

She walked on, but not before she had taken more photos of the police tape and open door.

What had they unearthed against Patrick?

It was too early for any of her ex-colleagues to be in the pub. Hannah bought herself a gin and tonic and sat at table with her back to the wall, where she could see anyone coming in. After taking a sip from her drink, she summoned up her courage to retrieve the piece of paper given to her in the Bull Ring. She smoothed out the crumpled paper. Scrawled in pencil were just four words:

You are being watched.

In a reflex action Hannah scanned the bar to see if anyone was looking her way. No one appeared to be even slightly interested in her. She thought back to her encounter in the Bull Ring. Was she being watched there? And if so by whom?

Hannah finished her drink and left, making for Blackfriars Road and the 63 bus home.

SIXTEEN

Hannah worked through the prints Rory had had developed from her hidden camera. Most of them taken during her trip through the Bull Ring after visiting Patrick, were too dark to properly make out the features of those she had been trying to capture but some were surprisingly clear. She placed those on the floor in a semicircle in front of her.

Six faces. What did she hope to gain from them?

Apart from the man who had given her the note, another tramp had been at the church when she'd discovered Fr Anthony was leading the service instead of Fr Patrick. She opened the envelope where she'd placed the polaroids Liz had taken of her clients. There he was again. Code-named Jonah. Jonah. Was the name randomly picked or did it have any significance? Did he choose the name or was it the one his parents had given him? Jonah. And according to the piece of paper given to her that afternoon, someone was watching her. Was it Jonah?

Hannah whose knowledge of biblical characters was sketchy at best, phoned Reverend John Daniels. He was out so she left a message and carried on organising the photos.

The phone rang. It was Reverend Daniels.

"Sorry Hannah I had a distraught parishioner with me when you rang. What can I do for you?"

"Tell me about Jonah."

"Jonah?"

"Yes what significance does he have? What does he symbolise?"

Revd Daniels chuckled. "Well you could easily read about him in the Bible, you know. It's only four short chapters."

Hannah remained silent.

"Ok. Jonah was the prophet who had disobeyed God by not following his command. God wanted him to go to the great city of Nineveh but Jonah did not want to go and set off in the opposite direction. He thought he could escape by sea but God created a terrible storm. Jonah knew that to save all the crew he would have to be sacrificed and so allowed himself to be cast overboard. The storm immediately calmed and Jonah was swallowed by a fish and held for three days before being released to do God's errand... Does that help?"

"I'm not sure really. You see all Liz's 'missionaries' as she liked to call her patients at St John's had code names. Jacob was found drowned in the Thames – I saw him outside the church that night and..."

"And you're clutching at straws."

"I suppose I am. I haven't a clue really. There's another man called Jonah. He was at the service when I'd gone to see Father Patrick. And I saw him when I walked through the Bull Ring."

"So?"

"So he doesn't seem to be one of them somehow. He's different."

"I think you'll find they are all different, Hannah. Each has his or her own story but they were all children once. And they are still

God's children now."

"Hmmm I was just wondering if there was any significance in the biblical connection. Maybe I'm just trying to find meaning where there is none."

"Well sorry I couldn't be of more help. Ring me again if you need to talk."

There were few women among Liz's clients. Hannah wondered why. She had seen plenty in Cardboard City. One who had spoken to her – Eileen if she remembered correctly – looked beyond Liz's ministrations – just a few teeth remained and they were yellowed from cigarettte smoke.

Hannah shuddered. The thought of losing teeth was the stuff of nightmares. Literally. She still remembered dreams in which she she spat out teeth as she rinsed her mouth. Anxiety. That's what those teeth dreams were supposed to represent. Unconsciously she ran her tongue over her upper front teeth.

Her attention was was brought back to the photo prints by a face staring back at her. There was something about him. He looked rough but the more she thought about it the more Hannah inspected the photo, the more it seemed to be "acquired". His demeanour seemed wrong. The clothes were dirty and tatty but somehow they didn't ring true. He looked like an actor playing a part but that was stupid. Even so she couldn't get rid of the thought. Her mind went back to a conversation she'd had with Liz soon after she'd started her "clinic".

"You wouldn't believe the stories of some of these people, Hannah. Sometimes just a freak set of circumstances and they are homeless and on the streets."

"I thought most of them chose to live that way without restrictions, out of society's grasp and all that."

Liz gave her an arch look. "I thought you of all people would be more understanding."

"Why 'of all people'?"

Liz busied herself by pouring them both more wine. They were each sitting on a sofa, legs stretched out before them, in Hannah's sitting room. Elizabeth had been tucked up in bed after being entertained by her namesake.

"Well after everything that happened last year. You took in that girl. Let her stay in your home, knowing little about her. Putting yourself and Elizabeth at risk…"

"Hey stop right there! I didn't deliberately put us at risk. It wasn't like that…"

Liz got up and hugged Hannah. She only knew part of the story. If she'd known all of it… "That came out all wrong. Sorry. It's just that that girl's story is so similar to some of those I hear."

"Don't keep calling her 'that girl'. Call her Caroline. That was her name."

"Yes but she had a working name too. Just like my clients using different names to cover up their pasts… And if you could see the people I worked with in Somalia." Liz stopped abruptly.

"You still haven't told me much about your time there. Why?"

"It all seems so unreal now." Liz concentrated on her wine for a few moments. "Going back to my homeless clients. They're not always what they seem, you know."

Hannah was aware that she'd been neatly diverted from Liz's time in the Somalian outpost where WelcAf worked from. Never mind she'd talk about it in her own time.

"Go on…"

"One guy had been a company director. Maybe that sounds too grand. But it was his own company that he'd built up over the years until he decided to sell up. He'd discovered his wife was having an affair with one of his employees and he was heartbroken. Anyway he sold up and, of course, paid a lot of money to his wife, ex-wife, and decided to emigrate to Spain. He bought a villa here, paid upfront, and then discovered, when he arrived, it was going to be repossessed by the government as the land had been leased only. He ended up with little money and what he did have he spent in bars… When he developed diabetes he didn't have the money for his treatment and eventually came back to the UK. He slept on friends' sofas and the quality of his life deteriorated until he found himself on the streets with nowhere else to go…"

"And how did he find his way to you?"

"Father Patrick encouraged him. He does a lot of outreach work in Cardboard City. He works really hard to get them help …"

"So how did you meet Father Patrick – not in Cardboard City?"

Hannah smiled at her friend and just nodded when Liz replied, "At some fundraising event."

Hannah brushed the tears from her cheeks. No more late night conversations over a bottle of wine with Liz. No more anything with Liz. She forced her attention back to the man in the photograph. She hadn't found him among Liz's clients' polaroids, so why did he seem so familiar? She couldn't put her finger on why exactly but he just didn't ring true. He looked as though he had assumed a part. And if that was the case, why?

So many questions. There seemed to be no motive behind Liz's murder. But there must be one. Increasingly Hannah felt the reason predated her time at the church clinic. She decided she'd take another look at the files on Liz's computer and a box of papers Lady Rayman had had sent over to her. Somewhere there were clues to this. Hannah was determined to find them.

But not tonight – she was far too tired. She missed Tom more than she would have thought and wondered yet again, why he hadn't phoned her. Feeling more alone than she would have thought possible she crept into Elizabeth's room and stared down at the sleeping toddler, mouth slightly open, one arm flung above her head, her breathing slow and steady. Hannah felt a rush of love and only just stopped herself picking up her daughter. Life went on. Elizabeth should always be her main concern.

SEVENTEEN

Hannah stood at the entrance to St John's waiting for the hearse and funeral cars to arrive. Fortunately the police investigation in the building was over very soon after it had started. No further information had been released to the press. The forensic search of the building was, apparently, part of ongoing investigations. Hannah had wondered if they had uncovered anything to do with Liz's murder and if they had, would they tell her? Probaby not.

The day should have been overcast, grey, but in defiance the sun's rays danced, shafted between buildings, refracted from every window. An explosion of light and optimism on such a day seemed a travesty.

She'd felt honoured when Liz's mother insisted she should be party to the cortége which would follow Liz's coffin into the church and sit with the chief mourners in the front pews. Now she wasn't so sure. Her legs felt weak. Her stomach churned. She scratched at her left hand and looked at her watch again. It was time. As she looked up the funeral cars swung into view.

The funeral director opened the car door and Lady Rayman emerged looking thinner, her expression held together by a lifetime of doing the right thing. Her pale olive suit echoed her grief. Mary, wearing a bright pink, followed her; the two women clutched at each other's arms. For a moment they paused each seeming or trying to draw strength from the other. Lady Rayman had asked everyone not to wear black. She wanted this to be a celebration of Liz's life. There were to be no flowers but donations to a children's charity. The only floral tribute was from Lady Rayman and Mary – red roses in the design of what was presumably the Rayman family crest.

The hearse drew up and the bearers assembled at the foot of the steps. The simple coffin was hoist on to their shoulders; each face bore an expression of extreme concentration as their burden tipped backwards when they climbed the steps.

Lady Rayman gripped Mary's hand as the coffin passed them and they formed the cortége in its wake. As they entered the church the priest pronounced the opening words:

"I am the resurrection and the life. He who believes in me will live, even though he dies, says the Lord."

As they made their way down the aisle, to the strains of Schubert, the whole congregation faced them. It was only later that Hannah realised Celia had hired a string quartet to play, and that piece was called "Death and the Maiden". The music hardly impinged on her consciousness as she concentrated on getting one foot in front of the other without tripping, willing her eyes to stay dry. The walk seemed interminable but in reality it must have been over within a few of minutes, their group was seated in the two front rows.

The service bore all the hallmarks of Lady Rayman's determination to highlight Liz's qualities and talents. Various friends some known to Hannah others not, participated with readings and memories. Then it was the moment for Hannah to deliver her eulogy. She felt Lady Rayman touch her arm gently then stood and walked the few steps to the rostrum. She took a deep breath as she took in the ocean of faces before her, unable to distinguish a single one as her sight blurred. Only afterwards did she realise that Liz's "missionaries" were sitting shoulder to shoulder with the Kensington set, the WelcAf representatives, and work colleagues.

"I feel so privileged to be able to make a tribute to Liz, my friend and confidante for only ten years, a moment in time compared to her relationships with some of you here… One of the interests we shared was a passion for poetry. We both loved Andrew Marvell so, in her honour, I'd like to read 'Mourning.'"

She swallowed hard and concentrated on the words before her. Fearing that tears would cloud her vision, she'd learned the poem by heart. But she still wasn't sure she'd get through it.

"You that decipher out the Fate

Of humane Off-springs from the skies …"

As she recited the lines she saw as though on a film reel visions of them together. Laughing, talking … hugging …

"Only to soften near her heart

A place to fix another wound."

That's how she felt. Wounded. Bereft.

"Nor that she payes, while she survives,

To her dead Love this Tribute due…"

All she could think of as she spoke these words were the lost opportunities, what they would never share. The silly misunderstandings that had developed in what neither could have known would be the last months of the friendship. Her voice broke as the last image of her dear friend threatened to overpower her. Then she looked at the photo she had attached to the poem. Of them together. Laughing as though there would never be an end to their mirth. Thank you James. She continued, "Would find her tears yet deeper ways…"

Hannah hesitated then found her voice: "I yet my silent Judgment keep." She ended the poem there. Three lines short. Knowing most people in the chuch would be none the wiser. She paused. Silent. She took a calming breath and looked across at Liz's coffin.

"Above all Liz loved life and she died doing something she so strongly believed in. Her compassion for others less favoured than herself … Her sense of right and justice was not prompted by any religion but by the special heart that beats no more … so many of us have reason to be grateful that we knew her and we will miss the light she brought into our world."

As she was leaving the rostrum, Hannah caught sight of a face she hadn't expected to see and almost stumbled before reaching her seat. Paul Montague was sitting towards the back, a few rows in front of Claudia Turner.

Hannah felt Lady Rayman's hand lightly touch her shoulder. "Thank you," she whispered.

The rest of the service passed in a blur for Hannah. All she could think about was Paul being there. Paul but not Tom. Hannah was furious with herself and with Tom. Why wasn't he with her now when her need was greatest. Some relationship this was if she was always on her own.

"We now commit Elizabeth's body to the ground;

earth to earth, ashes to ashes, dust to dust:

in the sure and certain hope of the resurrection to eternal life…"

It was over. Hannah stood and followed Lady Rayman as she and Mary led the way. Liz was leaving St John's for the last time.

Liz's final journey – to the crematorium – seemed interminable and lonely to Lady Rayman accompanied only by Mary, and they sat in mute grief. Mary had given up searching for words to communicate her loss and so, it seemed, had Lady Rayman. As the hearse and their car pulled in through the gates, Lady Rayman gripped Mary's hand so tightly her fingers felt they were melded together.

"I am so sorry, Celia. Maybe if…"

"No maybes, my dear. We did what we did. What we had to do. For the best. And it was for the best."

There was no ceremony. Celia and Mary read a poem from Wordsworth's Imitations of Immortality:

"What though the radiance which was once so bright

Be now forever taken from my sight,

Though nothing can bring back the hour

Of splendour in the grass, of glory in the flower;

We will grieve not, rather find

Strength in what remains behind"

and pushed the button together, staring wide-eyed but tearless at each other. Each pair of eyes reflected the other's sorrow. The curtain closed and they could hear the rumbling of the machinery moving the coffin to its final destination.

They left and the return journey to Waterloo seemed much quicker.

EIGHTEEN

The wake was to be at the back of the church which had a sort of kitchen and lots of space for tables of food. Hannah had been amazed that Lady Rayman had decided to hold the funeral as St John's – the scene of Liz's untimely and violent death – but she was adamant. The church, she had said, was not responsible for what had happened and she was convinced that Liz's mission there had nothing to do with her daughter's murder.

Lady Rayman had also arranged for caterers to deliver the buffet there so that the "down and outs" who had formed Liz's patient group at St John's would be able to stay and eat. Hannah knew that she had deliberately overcatered so that they could pack up the leftovers to be taken to Cardboard City. Liz's last gift to them.

Hannah stood in the church porch and watched Celia and Mary leave. As she turned back into the church, she walked straight into the bishop who had taken the ceremony. Hannah wondered why she was surprised that Lady Rayman had managed to get a bishop to preside at the funeral. With her connections it

and she was engulfed in his arms. For a few moments she gave way to the joy and comfort of his presence. Then he pulled back. "Sorry Hannah, have to get back to the Hammersmith. I'll see you later." As he kissed her on the forehead, she closed her eyes. Then he was gone and she saw Paul staring at James's retreating back. He glanced over at Hannah, raised his glass, and carried on talking to someone she didn't know.

For a moment she felt totally adrift. What the hell was Paul doing here? Was he really going out of his way to try and intimidate her. Don't give him the satisfaction of a reaction, she could almost hear Liz say those words to her. She turned away and saw that Claudia Turner was observing her from a few feet away.

Hannah made her way towards her. As she approached Claudia gave her what seemed like a sincere smile. "Well done, Hannah. That must have been difficult." She gave her arm a gentle squeeze. "And now I must get back to work." As if on cue her mobile rang. "Sorry I have to take this. When? Okay I'm just a few minutes away." Then she was gone.

"Excuse me, Hannah – hope you don't mind. Could we have a brief word?"

A tall, slim man, with a bronzed face and sun-streaked hair stood before her. He was probably a similar age to her – mid-thirties – and had the WelcAf logo as a badge in his lapel. "I'm sorry, I…"

"No I'm sorry. I was one of Liz's colleagues in Somalia – Sam Lockwood." He held out his hand. Hannah found hers gripped firmly. "I wonder if we could have a talk some time. Not here or now, of course. But it would be good to share some memories. And I understand from Lady Rayman you are going through all Liz's effects." Hannah nodded distractedly, looking over at the a group of the missionaries. "Liz was a great friend to WelcAf and I enjoyed working with her."

Hannah brought her focus back to him and smiled. He looked nice, enthusiastic. Charming. Hannah remembered her lapel camera and clicked. "Yes that would be good, Sam. Give me a ring – sorry there's someone I must have a word with." She handed him her card and moved way.

Celia Rayman and Mary were back and mixing with the funeral guests. Hannah watched how she treated everyone with the same equanimity. Mary was making sure the less fortunate among the throng were eating. She stopped and had a word with each one. Both women were circulating as though to the manor born and Hannah wondered how they managed to be so "together" for want of a better word.

Just then she felt someone tug at her sleeve. "Hello luv, my name's Lucy."

Hannah smiled. "Nice to meet you Lucy. I'm Hannah."

"I know that. Loved that poem you read. One of me sister's favourites." She smiled as if at some distant memory then switched back to the present. "And I know that you're a journalist, ain't you." Lucy coughed dramatically and took a glass of wine from a passing waiter. She took a large gulp.

"I was thinking it might be a good idea for you to come and speak to some of us down the Bull Ring." Lucy looked at her as if trying to judge her reaction. "Liz was very highly thought of, wasn't she. No one can understand what's happening."

Hannah's face must have reflected her skepticism. "Do you think anyone will talk to me, though?" she asked. "I did pass through the other day and was recognised by someone. That young man over there –" Hannah pointed him out – "he…

"Look," Lucy interrupted. "I'll meet you somewhere first. Then we'll go together. No one will think anything of it if you're with me."

Hannah smiled at the woman who was offering her protection – all five foot of her. Her grey hair stuck out in tendrils from her red, green and blue woollen bobble hat. Her jacket would have done Joseph proud with its multi-coloured stripes while her skirt seemed to pick up any colours that had been left out in other garments, daubed in various patterns on a black background. Her boots, however bucked the trend, and were a dull brown with scuffs and scratches, worn down at the heel.

"Okay when and where shall we meet?"

"What about the day after tomorrow so's I can ask around a bit myself? I'll see you outside Greggs bakers in Lower Marsh say four o'clock?"

"All right." Hannah wondered at the meeting place but said nothing.

"And just one thing…"

"Yes?"

"Don't wear anything posh like, you know. Find some old clothes so you won't stick out like a sore thumb."

Hannah smiled. "I'll do my best. And thank you, Lucy."

While she was considering what was really behind Lucy's invitation, Paul materialised beside her. "How are you bearing up?"

"As if you care."

"You'd be surprised." He gave her a long look and smiled but she was immune to his charms.

"Why are you here, Paul?"

"Like most people. To pay my respects, of course. I did know Liz."

Something in the way he said this jarred. "Yes, well I'm just going to say goodbye to Celia and Mary."

"Give my love to Elizabeth for me."

Hannah turned back to face him. "Do you know the meaning of the word? Or has Judy Burton been giving you lessons? Small world isn't it?" And she walked away before Paul could reply.

Drained by the experience of Liz's funeral, Hannah was grateful that Elizabeth had fallen asleep almost as soon as she put her in her cot. She ran a bath but as soon as she put one foot into it the phone rang. Tempted to ignore it she let the answerphone pick up then dashed into her study when she heard Tom's voice begin to leave a message.

"Tom, hi. Sorry I was in the bathroom."

There was that tell tale pause then, "How are you, Hannah? Today must have been very difficult for you."

"It was – for so many reasons."

"I wish I could have been with you."

"So do I." She was about to tell him about Paul being there, then decided against it. "A bishop conducted the service and… Tom he warned me not to meddle in things that don't concern me."

"Well that may have been good advice rather than a warning." Tom had already aired his disapproval of her involvement as such with Liz's murder.

"No it wasn't. He was referring to the priest who is in St Thomas's. But that wasn't the only thing. Before that he made an allusion to what happened last year he said Liz's death must have been hard for me so soon after… but he didn't finish his sentence. He just looked at me and it was… it was horrible. What does he know, Tom? And what's more how does he know?"

Hannah thought she heard a sigh then Tom's voice had the tone of a long-suffering teacher or parent. Not that of a lover who was concerned for her.

"Look Hannah, I think you're overreacting. Caroline's death was reported in the press. He was probably just thinking about her.

There's no reason to believe he knows any more. A coincidence, that's all."

"Don't patronise me Tom. I know what I heard and saw the way he looked at me. And to top it all the other day when I was at the Bull Ring, a tramp gave me a note telling me I was being watched."

"What? What on earth were you doing there?" She could tell Tom was losing patience with her. Well tough.

"I was looking to match up the client photos Liz had with the people who live there. Trying to make connections."

"Well maybe you should just leave that to the police. Claudia said…"

"Oh you've been in touch with her then."

"And what's that supposed to mean?"

"It means I hardly ever hear from you. You're not here when I need you but you have time for conversations with Claudia Turner!"

"Oh for God's sake! She's an ex-colleague. A friend. And she was worried about you as it happens." Tom's exasperation survived the transatlantic cables.

Hannah gulped the lump in her throat. At least he couldn't see her tears. She was furious with herself as well as Tom.

"Well, I'm worried for me, as it happens."

Sod's law there was some sort of commotion at Tom's end. "Sorry I'll have to go. Please take care." And with that the call ended.

Hannah's spirits sank even lower when she returned to the bathroom and lukewarm water. She turned on the hot tap but that soon ran cold. "Damn." *And damn Tom Jordan*, she thought. *Who does he think he is telling me I was overreacting? He hadn't been there. And he should have been if our relationship is going to have any meaning.*

As this thought took shape, it brought her up short. She had thought she and Tom had a future together. But what did she really know about him? He had saved her life. And Elizabeth's. But was that enough to carry them through his absence? She went to bed with that unhappy thought going round and round in her mind.

NINETEEN

"I'm so sorry to dump all this on you, Hannah," Celia Rayman had said, "but I really can't go through all these things myself. It seems such an intrusion of privacy."

Hannah had said nothing. She too would be intruding as Lady Rayman put it.

"Instead of filling your home with all this, could you come to Kensington to work through it and then take anything you might need to …"

Just before the funeral, Celia had found out that Liz had stored a whole load of boxes with her solicitor. These had now been deposited at the Rayman home.

"Of course, Celia. I'll come over tomorrow morning."

In the meantime there was something else she had to sort out.

Hannah walked into the charity shop when she thought it would be least busy. She had judged correctly. The place was empty and the woman sitting reading behind the counter looked a bit put out that she'd have to put down her book and attend to her.

"Good morning," Hannah said. "I wonder if you could help me? I'm looking for some clothes for a character I'm playing in a local amdram. I need to be a bit like a bag lady so I need stuff which looks as though it's seen better days…"

The woman with short white–blond hair and turquoise coloured glasses, smiled. "You know you're the second one I've had in here with a request like that. When's this play on?"

"Oh next month sometime, think it's the last week."

The woman gave her a "pull the other one" look but didn't push her for more details. "Actually you'd be doing me a favour if you took some of these rejects here. They're only fit for a jumble sale and perhaps not even that." She produced a laundry type bag from behind a door at the back of the shop. "I don't know how some people think we'd managed to sell this rubbish. I'm Jane by the way."

"Hannah."

"Right let's get stuck in, then."

After about half an hour they had between them put together a passable outfit for a bag lady.

When Hannah had tried on the skirt, jumper, coat and scarf she looked transformed. "I'll need a hat of some kind and some boots or shoes."

The footwear proved to be harder to find and eventually Hannah gave up and thought she had some old boots somewhere at home which she used in the garden. The wooly hat they found was perfect though and Hannah was able to tuck all her hair into it and still pull it quite far down on her face.

"How much do I owe you?"

"Just make a donation…"

Hannah handed her £10 which seemed to please Jane and they said goodbye, each pleased with their transaction.

Mary Cuthrington showed Hannah into a first floor room that was obviously rarely used in the Rayman household. Maybe it had once served as a dressing room as there was another door on the left hand wall but that now had a chair in front of it. There was another comfortable looking armchair placed by the window which looked out onto the gardens but little else in the way of furniture. Perhaps the room had been cleared to accommodate the boxes from Liz's solicitors.

She found herself surrounded by box files, envelopes and small boxes, wondering where on earth to begin. She had with her some empty trays and boxes ready to priotitise and tirage what she had before her. Mary Cuthrington had provided her with a pot of coffee and a plate of what looked like home-made biscuits on a tray and said she'd have lunch ready for her at one o'clock.

"You'll need a break from all this." She sniffed loudly. "Celia is out today so would you mind eating in the kitchen with me?"

Hannah had assured her it would be a pleasure and the companion left her to her task.

So much of what was in the first box, was of no interest whatsovever. Credit card receipts and bank statements. Hannah wondered why Liz kept them all. Perhaps it was for tax reasons. Hannah decided to concentrate on anything from the period that dated a few months leading up to when she left for Somalia until her return and death. A poignant reminder that the starting point was just after the time Hannah had told Liz she was pregnant. But that would have had no bearing on her friend's decision.

Three hours later, Hannah's mind was in a fug of inexplicable facts. She had discovered that Liz had started a trust fund for Elizabeth and she found various bits of paper with notes about what to buy Elizabeth for Christmas and her birthday. But one name which kept coming up was Kamaria Tuberkay. Liz had "adopted" her about five years previously. Regularly sent money for her education and to buy clothes. Kamaria's family was also included in this generosity. Hannah was stunned that Liz had never mentioned this to her. Did Celia know? She made a note to ask her in the pad she'd brought with her.

There was a knock on the door. Hannah called out to "come in".

Mary Cuthrington stood on the threshold but didn't enter. "Lunch is ready dear, if this is a good moment?"

Hannah smiled. "I could do with a break, Mary, thank you."

Thank you hardly seemed adequate for the trouble Mary had gone to for lunch. Soup, cold chicken, various salads with different dressings, jacket potatoes, some newly baked bread… "Goodness, this is a feast. You shouldn't have gone to so much trouble for me, Mary."

"Nonsense, you just tuck in."

They fell into a companionable silence. Hannah thinking about the papers. Mary, she noticed, eating very little.

"How long have you been here, Mary?" She remembered Liz saying she couldn't remember a time when Mary hadn't been with them.

"Must be some thirty-odd years now. Seems forever. And sometimes…" but Mary didn't elaborate.

"Did you know Lord Rayman? There are no photos of him anywhere except what appears to be a portrait of him as a very young man in the hall."

"Before my time, dear." Mary got up to clear the table. "But I hear he was a good father and husband."

"Then why would he just disappear?"

Mary shrugged. "Coffee?"

"Yes, thank you." Hannah stared at Mary's back. What was it Liz always said? "It's like having two mothers."

"I'll take it with me if that's ok?"

"Of course it is. I'll put it in a flask for you."

"Thank you, Mary, I could get used to this." She gave the older woman a hug and was surprised to see an unfathomable expression on Mary's face as she moved away.

"Just find something we can work on," was all she said but it cut Hannah to the quick. We.

Hannah returned to her boxes and worked solidly for the next few hours sorting and sifting. Instead of pouring over everything she thought might be of interest, she put those items to one side and was making much better progress.

When she next looked at her watch it was gone five o'clock and she would need to get home for Elizabeth. At least she could justify her absence by the fact that Celia was paying her. She put the documents she was taking with her into her briefcase and decided that she would leave everything else as it was ready for her next visit. She was just about to leave when Celia appeared at the door.

"Well, you've certainly made headway here, Hannah." She smiled but she looked tired and sad.

"I thought it would be ok to leave all this so I can pick up where I left off, probably tomorrow or the day after?"

"Of course it is. This is just one of the many rooms in this house that never get used…"

Hannah decided to broach the one subject that had intrigued her. "Celia… did you know that Liz had fostered a young girl in Somalia and regularly sent money?"

Lady Rayman looked puzzled for a moment. "No I didn't but that's just the sort of thing she'd do. And apart from her 'clinic' –"

Hannah could almost here the quotation marks around the word – "my daughter rarely spoke of her philanthropic works." She paused. "Anyway I mustn't keep you from your Elizabeth."

They walked to the front door together. "I suppose that's why she volunteered to work in that godforsaken place." Celia looked thoughtful. "To see the girl."

"Yes but she never mentioned her… at least not to me. And she never really explained why she returned so quickly, breaking her contract."

"Such a lot she kept to herself. Or maybe she told that priest she became so friendly with?"

"Perhaps," replied Hannah knowing it would be some time before Father Patrick would be able to remember much of value.

She kissed Celia on the cheek and was taken aback by her scent. The perfume was the same as Mary was wearing. Maybe they had lived together so long now their tastes had merged. Still, it made you wonder.

TWENTY

In the taxi going home, Hannah mulled over what she knew – or rather didn't know – about the absent Lord Rayman. Liz had been vague about when he left and what had happened between her parents.

"One day he was there and the next he wasn't. He wasn't one of those hands on fathers – hardly the fashion then – but I knew he loved me. I always felt loved. Even after he'd gone. For a while he'd send little gifts and cards but gradually they stopped…"

"But weren't you upset? Wasn't your mother?"

"Mummy was remarkably calm about the whole situation. Stiff upper lip and all that. She was never one for getting emotional and being all touchy feely. I suppose I just accepted the situation. I was only about three. It wasn't as if my daily life changed that much. We still lived in the same house, did the same things. Life went on – just without Daddy."

Now Hannah wondered if her father's disappearance had been the motivation behind Liz's work with the inhabitants of Cardboard City. Perhaps she thought that each vagrant she saw could be a link to her departed father? Did she stare into those Polaroids, searching for a likeness to Lord Rayman? And what about Jacob Gurnstein? What did he know which possibly cost him his life?

"'Ow far down Lordship Lane, luv?" The taxi driver's question brought her back to the present.

"Third on the left, thanks."

Hannah had the money ready in her hand as the cab pulled up outside her house. The driver had to stop in the road as in front of her gate was a vehicle she'd come to detest – a police car with the driver waiting patiently inside.

Hannah fumbled with front door keys and let herself in. The traffic from Kensington had meant she was later than expected but she certainly hadn't been anticipating a visit from Claudia Turner who stood up as she entered the sitting room.

"I'm sorry to disturb your evening, Hannah. But there have been some developments and I need you to come with me."

"Where?" Hannah still felt raw that Claudia had discussed her with Tom. And why? She felt betrayed by both of them but she really had no cause to expect any sort of loyalty from the inspector. Tom was another matter.

"St Thomas's. Patrick Ryan has regained consciousness."

"And?" Both women seemed awkward with each other.

"And he's asking for you?"

"Me?" Hannah was incredulous then irritated. "Why on earth didn't you contact me on my mobile? I passed the hospital on my way back from Kensington."

"I'm afraid that's my DC's fault… Anyway I thought you might need to arrange things here…" She left the sentence hanging.

Hannah left the room and ran up the stairs two at a time. Janet was bathing Elizabeth who sounded happy and contented as she went past the door to dump her breifcase containing Liz's documents in the study. The answerphone was flashing. Only one message from someone called DC Johns. Stupid man, why hadn't he had the sense to take down her mobile number and call her?

In the bathroom Hannah smiled at Elizabeth and felt a jolt of guilt for leaving her yet again. She had hardly spent any time with her today. Would it always be like this? The balancing act. She had known that whatever her circumstances she would never be content as a stay-at-home mother. Working freelance gave her more flexibility – the best of both worlds. And often it was but at the moment she seemed to have the worst of both.

"Janet, I'm really sorry but could you stay on for a while?"

Janet nodded. "It's not a problem. I thought you'd need me here longer so I let my mum know not to expect me at the usual time."

"Thanks." Hannah leaned into the bath and kissed Elizabeth's nose. "Bye bye gorgeous. See you later."

Elizabeth looked puzzled. "Bye bye Mama." Then: "No! No!" she wailed.

Janet immediately began to distract her with toys and bubbles. "You just go," she said. "She'll be fine."

Hannah was sure her daughter would be but she didn't feel fine. She felt wretched and confused as she went downstairs to find Claudia Turner talking into a radio phone; she sounded annoyed. She looked up. "Sorry about that. Are you ok to go now?"

"Do you know anything about Lord Rayman's disappearance?" DI Turner looked surprised. They were sitting together in the back of the car so it was easy to converse.

"Why do you ask?"

"Just fishing really. I wondered if Liz's preoccupation with the inhabitants of Cardboard City was linked to her father somehow.

She only told me that he left when she was a child and no one had seen or heard of him since."

Claudia looked thoughtful. "I did check him out, of course. But there was nothing of interest. No debts or scandal linked to his name. He just seems to have disappeared without trace and made a good job of it. That is if he is still alive."

"What makes you say that?"

"Well he'd be in his late sixties now. If he did take to the road it's not an easy life. Or maybe he went abroad. Still not my problem. Nor yours, I guess."

"True. Maybe whatever drove him away is best left buried."

"As indeed he may be." Claudia Turner smiled to take the sting from her words. But Hannah couldn't help thinking about Jacob Gurnstein and his death in the river. Did he have a family who have been mourning his loss for years? At least they would now have a body to bury... but maybe they hadn't been so heartbroken at his disappearance?

On the face of it Lady Rayman and Liz never showed signs of missing the husband and father they'd lost. There certainly didn't seem to be any financial hardship either. She assumed that Lord Rayman would have been declared dead after seven years and they would have had access to the family funds.

What different lives they'd led, she and Liz. And yet they'd had so much in common, or so Hannah had thought. Now she wasn't too sure. Hannah had always assumed they shared their thoughts and aspirations but not now. Liz's private papers showed that she hadn't needed to work from a financial perspective. And she had used a lot of her personal wealth to fund her activities in Somalia. So why had she left there so abruptly to return to her private practice in the Barbican?

"Penny for them?"

Hannah smiled. "I was just thinking about Liz. Why would anyone want to kill her?"

DI Turner was saved from answering a rhetorical question as the car pulled into St Thomas's.

"Let's see what priestly Patrick has to say, shall we?"

If that was an attempt at a joke, Hannah thought it was in poor taste, since the man had literally been unable to speak since he had been hospitalised. She felt a sick apprehension at what he might say now.

However they had only taken a few steps from the car when DI Turner's phone rang. "What? When did this happen?" She looked across at Hannah. "And you couldn't have alerted me earlier because..?" They had both stopped walking. "Make sure the officer guarding the room is fully appraised and meet me back at the station."

"I'm so sorry Hannah. Patrick apparently had some sort of seizure after he came round. Quite common in heroin overdoses, or so I'm led to believe. Anyway there was always a risk of major organ failure so the doctors have put him into an induced coma while they carry out more tests."

As she was saying this the DI held her arm and steered her back to the car. "My driver will take you home. I really am sorry…"

Stunned, Hannah sat in the back seat. There was nothing she could say except "Thank you" but what she was thanking the DI for was a mystery to both of them.

TWENTY-ONE

"Hi, it's Sam Lockwood."

There was a silence at the other end of the phone.

"We met at Liz Rayman's funeral. I worked with her in Somalia."

"Oh yes, Sam. Sorry I was in the middle of something and was miles away. What can I do for you?"

"I was wondering if we could meet up? I'm only in the country a few more days before I go back."

Something in the back of Hannah's mind urged caution. She couldn't pinpoint her anxiety but that sixth sense seemed to be working overtime these days. Especially since the funeral.

"Okay. Where would you like to meet, Sam?"

"I could come to you if that's easier?"

"No." Her abrupt response needed, she felt, more of an explanation. "No I've an appointment in town later. Whereabouts are you? We could meet somewhere convenient to us both."

They met in a small café, down a side street off The Strand.

Sam Lockwood was already sitting at a table and stood as she entered the room. It was, thankfully, warm inside but the windows were steamed up and, combined with the cigarette smoke, the café was clammy and uncomfortable.

"Hannah, good of you to come." Hannah sat down in the seat opposite him. "I've heard so much about you from Liz, that I feel we are almost friends already." He smiled and Hannah wondered whether he was one of what Liz had termed the misfits in Somalia. Or did he belong to the philanthropic group Liz had been part of?

"Well sorry but she never mentioned you." Hannah knew she sounded rude but she still felt raw from the funeral and the oblique warning the bishop had given her. "In fact she talked very little about her time in Somalia."

Sam smiled. "She was amazing out there. She had such compassion. Great with the kids. Everyone adored her."

"Then why did she return so abruptly?"

"I don't really know. There was some problem with local girls who went missing… I'm not sure how much Liz knew or thought she knew." Sam shrugged and stared into space. "Sometimes the heat, the disease and poverty get to you in ways you wouldn't expect."

"And do they get to you as well?" Hannah smiled and sipped the mug of coffee that had just been brought to their table.

"Sometimes. But I just felt Liz had other issues…"

"Really? What sort of issues?"

"I don't know exactly. Personal ones. She also came back with some files. Mainly day to day running of the outpost and that sort of thing. I telephoned Lady Rayman to see if she had them but she referred me to you. I understand you are sifting through all her correspondence and the like."

"I am – as and when the police are finished with them."

"Oh I thought they had returned everything." Peter made a show of concentrating on his coffee but Hannah knew he was watching her face for any clue to whatever it was he wanted to know. There was something about him that didn't ring true. And why should he know what the police had or had not returned? Unless Lady Rayman had told him which seemed unlikely to Hannah but she may have done.

"No. Not yet."

Sam sighed. "Oh well, perhaps you could post anything you find on to our London HQ?" He looked at his watch as though he was expecting someone or had to be somewhere else.

Just then Hannah's mobile phone rang. "Excuse me," she said as she stood and moved away from the table. "Right. I'm on my way," she said and finished the call.

She returned to their table and picked up her bag. "I'm sorry I have to leave now. Nice to meet you Sam, sorry I couldn't be of any help –" she held out her hand.

"Problem?" he asked.

It took all the skill Hannah had learned during interviews to look him in the eye and say, "None at all. Just my next appointment has arrived early." She smiled aware that he was staring after her as she made for the exit.

She walked down into The Strand and hailed a taxi.

Once inside she rang Janet to check she and Elizabeth were safe but there was no answer at the house so she assumed they were at one of their various toddler clubs. Her previous call had come from Celia Rayman. Her house had been burgled.

The police were very much in evidence when Hannah arrived at the Rayman residence. She was allowed into the ground floor sitting room where Celia and Mary were perched side by side on a sofa looking shell-shocked. DI Claudia Turner was sitting opposite them and a uniformed officer came in bearing a tray of tea.

All eyes were on Hannah who realised that whatever the burglars were looking for it wasn't antiques and fine art. The room seemed totally untouched. Perhaps it was.

"Hannah, dear, thank you for coming so quickly. I'm afraid the focus of whoever broke in was the room you were using to go through Liz's papers."

"Did you find anything interesting, Hannah?" DI Turner's tone was patronising to the point of rudeness. "Anything that might suggest why Liz was murdered?"

Hannah was appalled at the inspector's lack of sensitivity towards Celia who looked furious.

"No I haven't but you would know that as you would have had your officers go through everything first. I imagine they used a fine toothed comb." She allowed that comment to take effect. "I am just organsing things for Lady Rayman. Lots of the papers and files are of no interest to anyone and can be shredded. There are some which relate to her estate which will need to go to her solicitor."

"Did you know that your daughter had recently changed her will, Lady Rayman?" The DI's tone was far more conciliatory to the grieving mother.

"No I didn't Inspector but that shouldn't surprise any of us, knowing that she was pregnant at the time of her death." Lady Rayman's back was ramrod straight now. "I haven't seen the solictor yet as we need to be clear about all of the implications."

The DI inclined her head and changed tack. "Hannah would you come with me just to look at the room from the doorway to give me some idea of what the perpetrators may have done?"

"Of course." Hannah followed her out of the sitting room and up the sweeping staircase to the first floor room where Lady Rayman had deposited the files and boxes.

Hannah watched the scenes of crime team dusting for fingerprints.

"We'll need you to go through all this to see what's missing – if you have any idea, of course." Hannah couldn't understand why Claudia Turner was being so calculatingly cold after their previous conversations. Maybe she was just being professional in front of her colleagues? But in front of Celia and Mary as well?

"To be honest Inspector, I haven't even looked in all the files and boxes yet. It does look as though someone has been very thorough in their search, as boxes are open when I definitely hadn't even looked inside them."

Claudia Turner glared at her. "Quite." She surveyed the mess. "Anything strike you as unusual?"

Hannah parried the question with one of her own. "When did this happen?"

"Very early this morning I assume. The local nick received a call at around 7.30. Miss Cuthrington apparently noticed the door was ajar when she passed on her way downstairs to make breakfast…"

"How did they get in?" Hannah was still trying to process all the implications.

"Well, there was no forced entry. Do you have a set of keys to the front door?"

Hannah glared at her. "No I don't." She turned her attention to the room, trying to picture how she had left it. "I wonder what they were looking for?"

Claudia Turner echoed her thoughts as she too surveyed the scene. "Just what I was thinking. Do you think Liz may have brought back sensitive information? Maybe about WelcAf?"

Hannah didn't answer but asked, "Isn't it rather odd that whoever it was knew which room to go to?" She was really thinking out loud.

"It is, isn't it?" Claudia Turner's smile was not reassuring. "I'd like you to give the sergeant details of anyone you have told about what you are doing here. And we'll need your prints."

Hannah inadvertantly looked down at her fingers. "I don't recall telling anyone really."

"Well think about it. I've asked Lady Rayman as well."

Hannah was just about to dismiss the thought when she remembered a slither of conversation from earlier that morning: *"I understand you are sifting through all her correspondance and the like."*

"Sam Lockwood."

"I'm sorry?"

"Sam Lockwood knew. He worked with Liz in Somalia and said Lady Rayman had told him what I was doing."

"When was this?"

"At the funeral when I gave him my card. But I had a coffee with him today. He has my address ..."

Claudia Turner just managed to push her back onto a chair in the hallway. "Put your head between your knees." It was an order which Hannah obeyed. Everything went dark. She couldn't see. But she could hear Claudia barking into her phone. Then silence.

A glass of water was held to her lips. The darkness was evaporating but her fear was overtaking her, paralysing. Breathe, she told herself. Keep breathing.

"Hannah. Hannah can you hear me?"

Hannah tried to concetrate on the voice.

"Everything is okay at home. Elizabeth and Janet are safe. No one has been to the house. Can you hear me Hannah? They are safe."

"Thank God." Hannah unclasped her hand and saw blood. Her nails were bloodied too. "Sorry." She sniffed loudly. Someone handed her a tissue and she wiped her nose and hands. "Sorry, it's just…"

"No need to explain now, Hannah. I'll get a car to take you home." Hannah nodded her thanks. "Have you got any contact details for this Sam Lockwood?"

"In my bag. He gave me his card with the charity's HQ on it."

Claudia indicated to the PC nearby to retrieve the bag. "No need to worry Lady Rayman and her companion. We'll just get you home quickly."

Hannah rummaged in her bag for the card and handed it over to the DI. She stood up and leaned on the balustrade as she made her unsteady way downstairs. It was only when she was ensconced in the back seat of the car that she realised that even Sam Lockwood knowing what she was doing didn't explain how he or anyone else would have known which room she had been working in. But perhaps they'd had enough time to look in several rooms before hitting on the right one?

And how had Claudia Turner managed to check out her home so quickly? Presumably she'd contacted the local police station which was only a few minutes away. Or was her house under observation. And if so why? She was hardly a suspect. Her blood ran cold at the thought that Claudia Turner knew a lot more than she was letting on. Perhaps she thought Hannah might be under threat as well?

The shudder that thought sent through her body was like a powerful jolt of electrical current.

After the events of the previous year she had vowed she'd never put herself and her child at risk again. And yet, it seemed, she had done just that.

But she wouldn't, couldn't give up now. Liz had been killed for a reason – one which she was determined to uncover. Her appointment that afternoon might just throw some light on the situation.

TWENTY-TWO

Hannah managed to leave the house discreetly with her green holdall. The minicab was right outside her door so shielded her from prying eyes. As a precaution she had determined to go to Kings Cross Station first where she'd change into her charity shop clothes and leave her own clothes in the bag with Sam Smith in Lost Property.

She knew that Tom had had an arrangement with "Snapper" and was relying on his discretion. However she hadn't seen Sam since Caroline's funeral so was unprepared for his reaction when she'd visited him the day before.

"Why Miss, you're a sight for sore eyes." He beamed at her. The noise from the station was muted in here.

"Hello Sam, I wasn't sure you'd remember me." Hannah held out her hand but he came round from his side of the counter and gave her a hug. His limp seemed more pronounced but generally he looked in much better shape than the last time she'd seen him. But who looks their best at funerals? His prematurely grey hair was neatly trimmed. His shirt was pressed, and the jumper he was wearing looked expensive. Then Hannah realised it was home knitted. Obviously a work of love.

"You're looking good yourself, Sam." She smiled.

"I am, I am. Sit yourself down and I'll make us a brew." Hannah's heart sank.

"I don't want to put you to any trouble…"

Sam laughed. "S'alright I know you don't drink tea. I've got some coffee."

"You do? How?"

"Ah a certain mutual friend said that if I you ever came to me I was to give you any help you needed – and warned that you don't drink tea." This was all said from the little cubby hole to the left of the desk. Hannah surveyed the rows of shelves that disappeared into darkness housing the lost items which had been found but not claimed. A bedraggled teddy with one eye looked down on her and she wondered how long it had been there.

Sam limped back into view bearing two mugs. Hannah resisted the urge to relieve him of them before they spilled. It was surprisingly warm in the office and Hannah undid her coat buttons and loosened her scarf.

"Sit down, sit down –" he indicated the chair on her side of the counter. "So what brings you here, not that I'm not delighted to see you, of course."

Hannah felt guilty that her only reason was to ask for his help. She hadn't given him much of a thought since Caroline's funeral. But Tom had told her that Sam had been his snout and had given him valuable information. "He might be able to give you a story or two," Tom had joked.

Now here she was, perched on the chair in his office not knowing where to start. She wound a strand of hair around her finger. "Have you seen Marti and Gina recently?"

"Why?" Sam was evidently a master poker player.

"They were with you the last time I saw you at…"

"Princess's funeral," he finished for her. "Still can't think of her as Caroline. Poor kid. That was a bad business. But it's an ill wind…" Sam gulped his brew.

"Is it? Why?"

"Oh I'm just wittering on. Sorry. Yeah Marti's fine – finishes her degree this summer. And Gina, she's okay, I suppose. Still taking risks, silly cow."

It had amazed Hannah that Marti was financing her degree and bringing up her children with the money she earned as a sex worker. Marti confounded her. But she had helped Hannah discover what had been going on in relation to the murdered prostitutes.

Thinking about them brought Hannah close to tears as her finger worked a pattern on the countertop. Sam placed his hand over hers. "I was so sorry to hear about your friend, Hannah. Must've been a real blow for you coming so soon after…" He left the sentence unfinished. "I read your piece in *The News*."

Hannah nodded and swallowed hard.

"That's why I'm here Sam. I need a favour."

"Fire away."

"I was wondering if I could leave something with you for a couple of hours tomorrow?"

"'Course you can. You didn't need to come all the way here first to ask. As long as it's not hot and doesn't move." He laughed.

"No to both of those. I'll just look a bit different that's all."

"Don't say any more. What I don't know won't kill me." There was an awkward pause as he looked at her obviously appalled at what he'd just said. He finished his tea. "Heard from Tom lately?"

Hannah arrived at the King's Cross in plenty of time and made her way to the Ladies' toilets. It was a bit cramped trying to change in one of the cubicles without dropping items on to the none too clean-looking floor. She made sure she taken enough time in the cubicle for anyone who'd come in at the same time as her to have long left and went out to wash her hands and complete her transformation in front of the mirror. She removed her contact lenses and donned an old pair of glasses. The hat, which she found really itchy, concealed her hair and pair of holey gloves completed her look. She hardly recognised herself. And to be honest she didn't want to – looking like this she felt her sense of self plummet. She almost felt the way others would regard her – worthless.

The clothes were uncomfortable and smelled. She couldn't quite define the odour but it was a mixture of stale body odour, cigarette smoke, and many indefinable and probably unsavoury fragrances. She had been going to wash them before wearing them but thought the fresh smell of the clothes might give her away. She put everything she thought she might need into the many pockets she'd acquired with the coat. The camera was already discretely fixed to her lapel. Everything else went into the holdall which she clutched to her stomach as she made her way out onto the concourse and headed slowly towards her first test.

"Yes luv what can I do for you?" Sam looked up from his newspaper and his eyes showed no recognition.

"Could you look after this bag for a few hours, Sam?"

Sam stared hard, removed his glasses, wiped them on his sleeve and returned them to balance on his nose. "By the 'eck love, you've done a good job. Give it 'ere." He looked lost in thought for a moment. "We close at six." Hannah hadn't thought about the timings going back and must have looked crestfallen.

"Let's think – where are you going to be? Don't need the exact address," he said seeing her hesitation.

"Waterloo."

"Right. I'll take the bag and meet you in the Anchor – you know that pub in The Cut?" she nodded. "I'll be there from about 6.30 and I'll wait for you. Be careful." He returned to his newspaper as though uninterrupted. Hannah thanked him and passed him her business card with her mobile number. She'd decided, in case of emergencies, to keep the phone with her and turn it off while she was with Lucy.

One of the first things Hannah had noticed about the homeless was the sense of aimlessness. They walked slowly – they didn't have anywhere to rush to – so she made herself concentrate on reducing her speed which was amply helped by one of her old boots really pinching her toes, making her hobble. She made her way to the underground and took the Victoria Line to Leicester Square where she changed for the Northern Line.

She was aware that while no one looked directly at her, they inched away from her as though she were unclean and her poverty contagious.

With an immense feeling of relief she emerged from Waterloo station. At least her disguise seemed to be working. Meticulous as her preparations had been she still had plenty of time left before meeting Lucy so as the watery winter sun waned without any warmth she thought she'd go for a walk.

With a slight limp and hands stuffed in her pockets, she set off for St John's. The church was closed which wasn't unusual, she assumed, at this time of the afternoon and sat down on the steps. No one took any noticed of her. No one looked at her. She was invisible. In one way it was rather nice but she assumed that those who were really homeless would find that a further insult to their dignity.

She stood up – it really was too cold to loiter – and stamped her feet in a bid to activate her circulation. For want of something better to do she hummed to herself as she made her way down the road towards The Old Vic and crossed over the road to the right to Lower Marsh. The market stalls were long gone with only a few costers left packing away their wares.

She was at Greggs. "Hello Lucy," she said tapping her on the arm.

"What the fuck ¬– "

For a moment Hannah thought she'd been mistaken and it wasn't her. But then she caught sight of her face which was now grinning broadly. "Bloody hell – you've done a good job on yourself."

"I try to do as I'm told." Hannah winked. "Are you waiting for someone else?" she asked as Lucy showed no signs of moving.

"Yes won't be a mo."

A woman came out of the bakery wearing a blue nylon overall and carrying several largish bags. She was tiny with short hair styled in a tight perm and could have been aged anything from 45 to 65. "There you are Lucy love," she said, her gravelly voice and subsequent cough suggesting a heavy cigarette consumption. "I kept back a couple of yer favourites as well."

"Thanks Kit, you're an angel."

The woman from the shop coughed loudly acknowledging Hannah with a half-smile. "Aint seen you around here before."

"Nah," said Lucy. "She's on 'er 'olidays. Usually resides at the Cross."

The two women burst into cackles of laughter and then Lucy linked arms with Hannah and they ambled along to the Bull Ring.

"Nervous?" Lucy asked.

"I am a bit. I feel a fraud dressed like this as though I'm trying to deceive people."

"You'll be glad you did, my girl. You'll be more or less accepted as you are. No one asks questions. We'll just mingle a bit and see who we can see…"

Hannah drew confidence from the other woman. Lucy had been around long enough to know the ropes. But there was a tiny worry at the back of her mind that she might be being set up.

TWENTY-THREE

Sights and sounds but not smells were muted as they descended into the Bull Ring. With Lucy by her side, she was absorbing the atmosphere in a very different way. It took a while for Hannah's eyes to adjust to the pale dimness. It occured to her that she'd never seen so many different shades of grey. Everything was grey apart from the yellowness from the lights at periodic intervals. Lucy led her to what appeared to be a cardboard tunnel which was in fact her home where she slept and stored her few possessions when there was someone she could trust to keep a watch on them. Hannah activated the recorder in her pocket unsure how much it would pick up.

"Thanks Ben." Lucy handed the bag to the man whom Hannah hadn't seen before. "Choose your poison."

Ben picked out a filled roll. "Thanks Lucy me girl. That'll go down a treat. I'll push off for a while. See you later."

The man at the next box looked across and Hannah had to stop herself staring at the real face of one of the polaroids in Liz's box. "Anything for me in there Loos?"

"Play your cards right there is."

The man moved nearer. There was something about him… "What the fuck are you playing at?" He spat the words into her ear as he reached for Lucy's bag.

Hannah could feel her colour rising but managed to use her concealed camera before his hand gripped her wrist so tightly she thought she'd faint with the pain. "Let go of me!" Her voice was louder than she intended. As Lucy saw what was happening she gave him a deft kick in the shin.

"Paws off, you big tosser. This is a friend of mine. Leave her alone or you can piss off."

Strangely Hannah saw no animosity in his eyes. He let go of her wrist which she rubbed gingerly.

Lucy continued as though nothing had happened. "We were just remembering the lovely Liz. Such a bleeding shame. And why would any of us want to do her in? I tell you the pigs have got arses for brains."

"Is that what they're saying," said a voice emanating from the shadows beyond. "Do they think it was one of us?"

"They do, Beano. Just another bloody cover up if you ask me."

What Hannah had never noticed before as she had walked through here on her way to work was the level of noise. It was a constant barrage of sounds. A man playing a mouth organ, someone snoring, a heated argument, someone muttering to herself, a dog whining, someone sobbing, a tattoo being beaten with sticks on a tin. A cacaphony of sounds which was grating and reassuring at the same time.

"And what do you think, Sherlock?" Lucy was addressing the man who had grabbed her.

"I think we're best off not getting involved." The man concentrated on his sandwich.

"Oh really." Lucy's voice was cutting. "That's why you've been nosing around asking questions is it?"

Hannah stared at him. Willing him to say something, anything which might make her time here worthwhile. She accepted a roll from Lucy's bag feeling a complete fraud. But if she'd turn it down, she might have fuelled the suspicions of the man called Sherlock even more.

"You don't want to pay attention to him. He's full of shit, he is."

"Piss off, Grady. Remember Jacob. He ended up in the fucking river for his pains." This was Sherlock again.

Hannah was about to ask why Jacob had been asking questions when she saw Lucy's slight shake of the head. From the recesses of her shelter, Lucy brought out some cans and handed them round. Hannah was about to decline but then thought that again would draw the wrong kind of attention.

"And Father Patrick. Who got at him? Bastards."

"Anyone hear how he is?" This was Beano asking.

"Not good I hear."

"Oh yeah and how d'you hear that, Sherlock?"

"I have my sources." He looked straight at Hannah. "And there was someone sniffing around the church the day before Liz died. Asking questions. Being nosy."

"What sort of someone?" Lucy asked.

Sherlock shrugged. "A suit. They all look the same."

"So who did he speak to then?" Lucy was looking daggers at Sherlock.

"Your guess is as good as mine." Sherlock lit a roll-up and inhaled deeply. "Someone who likes some cash in their hand."

"Don't we all," mumbled Eileen, the woman who'd confronted her on her previous sally into the Bull Ring but without her disguise.

By now they were all on their second can. Hannah had only sipped at her first one. She thought she'd got away with it until she realised Sherlock was staring straight at her again. This had been a foolish idea.

"Maybe some reporter ought to come down here and flash the cash," he suggested.

"And what would you say then Sherlock you big fraud?" Lucy passed him another can.

"I'd say there's more to this than meets the eye. Maybe Liz's murderer had followed her from that Godforsaken place she was working in Africa."

"Why would you say that?" Hannah was intrigued. She had slowly been coming to that conclusion herself.

"Stands to reason. Strange things happen when you're away from home."

"And you'd know that, wouldn't you," said Beano more into his can than to Sherlock.

"What I'd like to know is what's happened to Jacob. No funeral I suppose. Straight to the bloody incinerator." This came from Eileen.

That question had occurred to Hannah as well and she made a mental note to ask Claudia Turner.

Sherlock grunted and concentrated on his beer but she sensed he was still watching her, scrutinising her.

Hannah was aware that there was and had been for some time an increase in the number of people passing by. Commuters making for the station to go home. It was like an inner circle of speed against the slow machinations of Cardboard City. Two parallel worlds. It had turned much darker and colder. A few of the rough sleepers had little camping stoves that threw off some warmth while they heated food most of which seemed to come out of tins. Convenient convenience foods.

Lucy got to her feet a triffle unsteadily. Ben had returned and was handed a can. "Right I'm off for me constitutional." She touched Hannah's arm. "Come on luv."

And with that the ordeal was almost over.

"Who's the guy you called Sherlock, Lucy?"

"Dunno, really. He turned up a few months ago, I suppose. Full of himself, that one. Still live and let live."

"Do you know anyone called Jonah?"

Lucy seemed lost in thought. A strange expression crossed her face in the changing light from the Bull Ring to the world above ground. "Jonah? He's gone up in the world selling that *Big Issue* magazine over the water."

Hannah smiled at Lucy calling the Thames the water.

"Thanks for today, Lucy. You've been a great help." Hannah passed her an envelope containing cash *The News*, courtesy of Rory, had given her.

"I don't want yer money. I didn't do it for that." Her mouth was set in a determined line.

"I know you didn't but you might as well take it. It's not my money, it's the newspaper's. Do what you like with it." Hannah smiled her encouragement.

Lucy took the notes out of the envelope and stuffed them into various unseen pocket within her various layers of clothes. "Ta love. Look I'll keep me eyes and ears open. I've got your card. I'll phone if I hear anything. And you can always get to me through Kit at Greggs. I go there every day except Sundays at the same time to collect what they haven't sold. She'll take a message for me."

She stopped walking abruptly. "Right I'll love you and leave you now. " She took Hannah's hand. "Look after yourself love and be careful for gawd's sake."

Sam was waiting for her in the Anchor. He was drinking a pint and there was a brandy waiting for her. "Thought you might need that."

"Thanks, Sam." Hannah sipped her drink and looked round at the drinkers. It wasn't a pub usually frequented by the IPC crowd and she was relieved not to recognise anyone.

"This has been so good of you." She reached into her holdall and gave him an envelope.

"What's this? I hope you're not going to insult me by…"

She leaned forward and kissed him on the cheek. "I'd never do that, Sam. This is newspaper cash. Take it." He hesitated, his conscience fighting a losing battle as he tucked the envelope into his inside coat pocket.

"Would you mind walking me outside to see if I can get a cab home?"

"Course not." He finished his drink and stood up.

Sam held her elbow as they made their way through the mass of post work drinkers none of whom even glanced her way, out onto The Cut. He managed to get a cab straightaway and bundled her into it before the driver could get a look at her.

"Keep in touch, Sam. You have my card." He nodded but his expression in the light of the streetlamp looked immeasurably sad.

The driver did a u-turn after she gave her address and she whipped off the itchy hat allowing her hair to cascade out. She also changed her boots and coat so that she looked somewhat more of her old self by the time she reached home.

Janet was just putting Elizabeth to bed but she didn't want to be near her daughter before getting rid of the stink she'd aquired. Stripping off in the bathroom, she took a hot shower, scrubbing her skin and washing her hair twice. She wrapped herself in her bathrobe and her hair in a towel before gathering all her jumble clothes and thrusting them into a black bin liner. She hoped she wouldn't need to wear them again but she couldn't deny their discomfort had been worth it. She scrubbed her hands again and quickly applied some cream before creeping into Elizabeth's room.

Janet was humming a lullaby and looked up and smiled. Hannah felt both reassured and jealous. Elizabeth's eyes opened momentarily and locked on to her mother's. The infant sighed with sleepy contentment and the two women left the room.

TWENTY-FOUR

The next morning Hannah sent the camera back to Rory by courier and while she was waiting for the prints listened to the recording she'd made. It was next to useless. It picked up all the background noise but none of the conversation which Hannah now jotted down from memory and played with a memory map and colours. Liz's name was in the middle. The links coming out were Fr Patrick, Lord Rayman, Lady Rayman, the charity WelcAf, St John's, baby's father, Jacob Gurnstein, Jonah, Sherlock, police.

Hannah underlined WelcAf. What had taken Liz there and what had made her return in the way she did?

She stared out onto the winter garden. Everything was bare. A pot had been blown over. A brightly coloured ball looked like an artificial flower in the frost-hardened earth. Hannah detested the winter months and more so now that it was the season of Liz's death. She still found it hard to believe that she would never be seeing her friend again. Sometimes it seemed as though she had just gone off to another charity somewhere and they would meet up again.

However at that moment for Hannah Liz's absence was a physical pain. She tried not to think what Liz's last moments had been like. She clutched at her grief and wrapped it round her so tightly that it threatened to engulf her entirely. Then she heard her daughter's shriek of laughter when Janet said some silly nonsense to her as she strapped her into the buggy. It brought her back to the present, to life and love.

It seemed no sooner had they left the house than someone rang the doorbell. Hannah went downstairs and looked though the spy hole before she opened the door. James was standing there holding a bunch of snowdrops.

"Hi. I just thought I'd call by to see how you are. Sorry I should have rung first, I didn't think. When I get some time off I assume everyone else is at my disposal." He grinned sheepishly. "Bad timing?"

"No of course not, come in it's freezing out there."

James seemed to fill the narrow confines of the hall and Hannah stepped back. "Shall I take your coat?"

James handed her the flowers before shrugging off his duffle coat. He followed her into the kitchen as she went to find a vase. "Coffee?"

"Yes please. Where's Elizabeth?"

"Janet's taken her to the park. She won't be long in this weather." She arranged the snowdrops into a vase as the kettled boiled. "These are lovely, thank you. My favourite winter flower."

James was quiet staring out into the garden. Hannah handed him a mug of coffee. "In here or the sitting room?" he asked.

"Sitting room is more comfortable."

"So how are you," James asked once they were ensconced on sofas.

"Getting there. It's weird going through all Liz's papers and things."

"Why are you doing that?" James looked bemused.

"Lady Rayman asked me to. She's… she's paying me to look into the circumstances around Liz's death."

James made no comment. Unlike Tom she thought who had been loud in his criticsim of her – and indignant.

"I assume she thinks I'll be more sensitive to anything I may discover. Especially concerning the media interest."

"You still with that rag?"

"You know I am. I have a contract and they pay me a retainer. Not that I have to do much for that. Just turn up for the odd editorial meeting and write a piece when they ask me to."

James stared at his coffee. There were no revelations but he looked as though he'd come to a decision when he looked up at her.

"Would you have dinner with me?"

Hannah stared at him for a moment. "I'd love to. D'you mean this evening?"

James nodded. "Bit short notice but –"

"No it's a lovely idea but I've imposed on Janet quite a lot recently and she's leaving early this afternoon. So may I suggest a takeaway here? Would you mind."

"Not in the least." He drained his coffee. "What time shall I come back?"

Hannah felt a buttlerfly colony had invaded her stomach as she changed her dress before James was due. They had known each other for such a long time and he had been so good to Caroline. But they never really spent time alone together. She wondered why. She also wondered why some woman hadn't grabbed him by now. He was intelligent, fun when he wasn't being too serious. Attractive. No not just attractive, he was gorgeous. Hannah paused mid application of blusher. She stared at herself in the mirror. Why had she never noticed that before? Paul probably. Then she was pregnant. Then Elizabeth. Then Tom. When all the time James had been there.

She laughed. "And what makes you think he has any romantic interest in you, Hannah Weybridge, huh?" she asked her mirror image.

Her reflection said nothing but replied with a wink.

Always one for punctuality, Hannah's first thought when the doorbell rang at a quarter past eight, was, *He's late*. She opened the door with a flourish and there stood James looking his beautiful self and carrying bags from one of the local Indian restaurants.

He smiled as he stepped into the hall. "Thought I'd get this en route. I have a selection which I hope will meet with your approval, ma'am."

Hannah took the bags as he took off his duffle coat. She had already laid the table in the dining-room and had opened a bottle of red wine which she knew he preferred. The snowdrops he'd bought earlier took pride of place in the centre of the table.

They sat facing each other. Waiting. Hannah broke the silence. "Shall we tuck in before this feast gets cold?"

As they helped themselves to green chicken handi, rice, dahl, chana massala, naan bread and onion bahjis, they chatted easily until James asked, "Have you come up with any leads on Liz's murder?"

"I'm not sure really." Hannah sipped her wine. "I'm convinced her death has something to do with her time in Somalia."

"Why so?"

Hannah paused to consider her reply. "She was deeply upset by how the girls were subjected to FGM. Female Genital Mutilation."

"I know what FGM is, Hannah."

"Sorry." Hannah helped herself to some more curry. "She went to Somalia, I think, because she had 'adopted' a girl there and was sending her money regularly."

"Can't see that would be any reason to murder her."

"No I could be way off beam here. But I would like to interview someone about FGM. I wondered if you knew anyone I could ask?"

James looked furious. "Are you asking me because I'm black Hannah?"

"No of course not." Hannah had the grace to blush. Until recently she had never given much thought to James's colour or origins. She had never actually thought of him as black. His pale coffee coloured skin and dark hair reflected his mixed heritage.

"I was born here, Hannah. My father came here as a young adult. For God's sake I'm more likely to know about what's going on in China than I am in Somalia."

"I'm sorry, James, I didn't mean to offend you. I actually thought you might have had some connections via the hospital."

He sighed theatrically. "Well, I do have some people I could contact and ask a few discreet questions."

"Oh would you? James you're a hero."

"I'll see what I can do. No promises, okay?"

"Okay." Hannah lowered her eyes so he wouldn't read in them the triumph she felt.

"More wine?"

"No, I'd better make tracks. Early shift tomorrow."

Hannah felt as though she'd been slapped in the face. She could have kicked herself. James obviously thought she was using him and sadly she was. "You won't forget..?" she asked as he put on his coat in the hall.

He pulled her to him in bear hug.

"No I won't forget."

The trouble was what she couldn't know – what he didn't want to remember.

Somalia May 1993

Dear Hannah,

I wonder where you are when you are reading this? Where will I be? Actually I hope you never open this letter because that will mean that things have worked out and I am safe.

Sometimes I wonder if I'll ever be safe again. This place is terrifying. The people here are never what they seem to be. Whom can I trust? The answer is no one. Hannah I am scared for my life. I came here with such good intentions and hope. Hope that I would be able to do some good. Hope that I'd make a difference, however small. And hope that I would be able to find Kamaria and her family. Her name means "like the moon". Tragically she will never see that moon again.

You may or may not know by now that I "fostered" Kamaria. You know the type of thing – standing order once a month that satisfies the the charitable do-gooder in us without having to actually do anything. Letters every now and again telling the sponsor how the child is doing etc. But somehow they – Kamaria's family – got other letters to me. She had been raped by an uncle and, it transpired, traded into some "terrorist" organisation. I had to come here and see what was happening. By the time I arrived Kamaria's family had also disappeared. Moved on – no one seemed to know where. It seems unlikely. Where would they go to? Unless they too had been taken or killed by the terrorists.

No one is saying anything although somebody must know something.

So here I am in this godforsaken place. Everything is so basic you wouldn't believe. No sanitation or running water means people have to leave their hovels (no other word to describe them) when they want to pee etc. When this happens in the night the girls and women are at their most vulnerable. Kamaria was just eight years old when she was raped. Can you believe it?

The charity workers here live in conditions that are hardly any better although we do have armed guards patrolling the perimeter of our compound. And a high fence – not sure if that's to keep us in or others out. We have very basic sanitary conveniences that are a million times better than what the villagers have. Plus we have an electricity generator which doesn't always work but does fulfill some function.

The trouble is I have to be on my guard the whole time. It's exhausting but if I confide in anyone I may put others at risk. No one here knew about my connection with Kamaria and her family. It was just as well.

Hannah I'm scared. There are people here who are trafficking young girls. They just disappear. I try to keep meticulous records of families I see. Most of the time I am employed in teaching basic hygiene – and I don't mean orally. I have established codes and cross-referencing. Trying to keep track of the girls. But I have to be so careful. I think some of the charity workers here are involved. I'm not sure who or how many but it makes me sick to death.

I feel I must come home earlier than planned. I've stayed here too long already. People are beginning to question some of my actions. God knows why. Maybe guilty consciences.

Anyway I hope you never read this. I trust when I return I can try to establish the truth of what is going on here and expose the perpetrators. I'll need your journalistic help then. Maybe we can do this together. Maybe…

I've had to find a way of hiding anything I write as I am sure someone is going through my papers. A horrid thought but I've learned to be careful. I always know when someone has been in my hut. Amazing what you can do with dental floss!

TWENTY-FIVE

Hannah put the letter down. Her whole body felt leaden. She was terrified. If Liz's murderer or murderers were connected to the charity in some way then it could be she too was at risk now that she was in possession of some of Liz's documents.

She decided to photocopy anything that could be incriminating and send copies to people she could trust. Revd John Daniels and James. The decision reminded her of Caroline's diaries. However she hadn't read those before they were sent. She would take the added precaution of storing another set – and she knew just the place. Hide things in full view and they won't be seen. She was sure Sam at King's Cross would help her – especially if he had no idea what the parcel contained.

She would also ask Rory if the news desk had had any reports of trafficking in Somalia that could be connected with the charity.

She should visit the charity HQ. They needn't know she had any information on Liz's time there but she could ask about Kamaria, saying she'd found a bequest in a codicil to Liz's will. That might work. Or not. Be brave, she told herself. But she didn't feel brave and wondered how much she could or should tell DI Turner. What she needed was a contact in the Foreign Office. And she was more likely to find someone via a broadsheet rather than *The News*.

However she could use the library at *The News* and check though the cuttings library and the microfiche files. That would be a start.

Hannah was surprised when she saw the entrance for the WelcAf's head office. It was a door with peeling paintwork at the side of a burger café just off Hammersmith Broadway. She'd taken the tube from Westminster and on the way went over in her mind what she would ask. She'd made some notes on her pad. Having phoned ahead she'd mentioned her connection to Liz Rayman and said she was looking for background information for an article she was writing for *The News*. So far, so true. Seeing the entrance to their offices, she was relieved that at least they weren't spending any money they raised for their charitable work on their own comfort.

A voice answered her ring on the bell and when she gave her name a buzzer sounded and she pushed the door open to reveal a narrow and steep flight of stairs. The faded blue walls were covered with campaign posters some of which were now faded and curling at the edges. Hannah clutched at the handrail and counted the steps. There was only one way to turn at the top – right – which she did and pushed open another tacky door with a square of glass positioned at about head height.

"Hi Hannah – I'm Cheryl otherwise known as general dogsbody here." The mousy haired girl with wire-framed glasses held out her hand.

"Nice to meet you Cheryl." Never had anyone looked less like a Cheryl, thought Hannah. The name, for her, conjured up a sophisticated and glamorous being. This one was wearing a huge red cardigan over thick leggings in a sickly shade of green that ended with her feet in Doc Martens. Every finger including her thumbs bore a ring and a small tattoo peeped over her collar. Whatever her appearance, she seemed genuinely friendly.

"I was so sorry to hear about Liz. She was doing such good work out in…"

The inner door opened to reveal a smartly dressed – dapper was the word that leaped into Hannah's mind – man who could have been aged anywhere in his forties or fifties. "Ms Weybridge I presume? Michael Dresden, CEO of WelcAf."

Hannah shook his hand. "It's really good of you to see me at such short notice, Mr Dresden."

"Not all – and please call me Michael, Hannah. We were all devastated when Liz died. Please – " his hand indicated his office. "Could you drum up some coffee for us please, Cheryl?"

The door closed on whatever Cheryl's answer had been.

Hannah took the chair indicated. Unlike it's occupant, this office was drab and tatty too. Michael Dresden's desk was a maze of piles of paperwork, proofs for campaign leaflets, files in various colours. Adorning the wall behind the desk was an enormous map of Africa with coloured flags pinned into it. Hannah assumed that's where they had their outposts. Geography was not her strong point but she now knew exactly where Somalia was and where Liz had been stationed. The position was marked with a series of red and yellow flags. She wondered at the significance of the colours.

Michael Dresden perched on the corner of his desk and leaned forward to open the door as Cheryl came in with two coffees on a tray with milk and sugar. Hannah took hers black.

"Now what can I do to help you." The CEO added milk and two sugars to his cup.

Hannah smiled. "I'm just after a bit of background information really. For instance I was wondering whether Liz contacted you directly or through a third party when she volunteered? As you're not a major player I mean. I hadn't heard of you, I'm sorry to say."

"No that's par for the course really. We do our best with limited resources. However we are an international organisation but sadly our London office is really small fry. Sometimes we piggy-back on other charity recruitment events. But to answer your question, Liz was referred to us by another organisation who knew of us and thought Liz would make a good match."

"Why was that?" Hannah sipped her coffee.

"We do a lot of outreach work in Somalia and that's where Liz wanted to go."

"Was she that specific?"

"Yes, she was as a matter of fact. I thought it curious at the time but finding candidates for any area we work in is hard enough so we just jumped at her offer. She had the funding all sorted so there was no hassle with raising the necessary money as there usually is."

Hannah smiled. "Do you know why she returned to the UK before her term finished?"

Michael Dresden shrugged. "I've no idea. However if other early returnees are anything to go by it's usually charity fatigue. Our outreach camps are basic. The terrain is often unforgiving and the weather can be equally so. I must say it was unsual for a woman to sign up for such a long stint anyway. We did our best to point out all the drawbacks but she was adamant."

"Sounds like Liz." Hannah sighed. "Did she make any particular friends while she was there?"

"That I don't know but you did meet Sam Lockwood at Liz's funeral. Not sure how friendly they were but the expats aren't numerous so they would have socialised if you can call it that."

"How many charity workers do you actually have there?" Hannah asked glancing out of the window. The view was of unremmitting backs of buildings with their fire escapes and a spaghetti junction of gutterings and downpipes.

"Actually I've put together a file of info for you. Just about everything we have about the camp and personnel." He handed Hannah a yellow file.

"That's very kind of you." Hannah took this as her cue to leave.

"Vested interest. I know it's only background material for your article but any publicity can help raise our profile." He smiled and shook her hand. "I am very sorry for your loss Hannah. I did write to Lady Rayman but what can one say…"

"Indeed. Thank you for your time."

"I would say it's a pleasure but given the circumstances... Take care Hannah. Goodbye." He closed the office door behind her. Cheryl looked up and handed her an envelope.

"I think this may help too. Good luck Hannah."

Hannah tucked the envelope into the file and put it into her bag.

"Thanks Cheryl. How long have you worked here?

"Eighteen months. I started after being active in the field. Supposed to be a stopgap but I'm still here?"

"Would you go back into the field?"

"Never." Hannah thought she caught an expression of despair on the other woman's face. But it was fleeting. "Never," she said but this time with a sad smile.

On her way home Hannah made a detour to King's Cross. She had a package ready to leave with Sam. As she approached the Lost Property office, she could hear low voices and then laughter. Hesitantly she walked in and saw Marti sitting in a chair – knitting

– while Sam regaled her with some story. *Well that explains the smart jumpers*, Hannah thought.

Marti jumped up and surprised Hannah by hugging her. "How are you?" she asked. Then said, "Don't answer that stupid question. I'm sorry Hannah."

"Well better for seeing you, that's for sure." Hannah smiled. "Sorry to interrupt but I need to get home and I just wanted you to hold this for me, Sam."

Sam took the jiffy bag and limped down one of the aisles, returning empty-handed.

"Thank you."

"Don't be daft, I told you before as long as it's not hot and it doesn't move… It's not hot is it?" He was smiling at Marti.

"No. But I do need it to be kept safe."

"Best place then," said Sam. "Sure you won't stay for a coffee?"

TWENTY-SIX

"Did you and Liz fall out about anything?"

Hannah looked up in surprise at Lady Rayman's question. They were in the makeshift office now that the police had finished with it, sorting though boxes. Celia had decided to help her for some reason. Now Hannah wondered if there was an ulterior motive. She felt compelled to answer as honestly as she could. "We didn't always see eye to eye. And I felt there was a certain coolness between us when I became pregnant. I think Liz probably got fed up of my hormonal swings and one track mind." Hannah smiled ruefully.

"Oh do you think so? I thought she was rather excited for you."

"Excited for me but probably bored for herself. I felt that was one of the reasons she went off to Somalia."

"Mmm perhaps. We'll never know now. I wonder what sort of mother she would have made?"

A single tear traversed her cheek and dropped onto the sheet of paper she was reading. Hannah had no idea what it was that Lady Rayman had found. But the question about her relationship to Liz made her shudder. She'd always thought they had been so close.

Now all that she'd cherished about their friendship had seemed to unravel with Liz's death.

Hannah took a deep breath to ask the one question she was aching to know the answer to, "Do you think Liz was searching for her father?"

Celia Rayman's face was a mask of impenetrability. "What on earth makes you think that?"

Hannah held her gaze. She could see where Liz got her inscrutability from. "I'm sorry. I don't wish to offend you Celia but I wondered if Liz worked in her clinic at St John's in the hope of discovering more about her father... as he had disappeared I thought maybe he had taken to the road..." Hannah's voice tailed off in embarassment but when she looked again at Lady Rayman she was smiling.

"Good Lord, no. Liz knew what happened to her father. There was no need for her to search for him."

"Oh." Hannah couldn't think of anything else to say. She wanted to ask what had happened to Lord Rayman but she knew from his wife's expression that that question would be as unwelcome as to her ears it was inappropriate.

"Why do you think she worked with them then, the down and outs and homeless? It can't have been an easy call." It made Hannah feel queasy just thinking about the state of some of those mouths full of decay and dirt. How could Liz have delved into cavities and caries and not felt her stomach heave? She must have been tougher than Hannah ever gave her credit for. But then she must have had an inner strength that took her off to Somalia. Who in their right mind would volunteer to go there?

Hannah thought of the young woman in the charity's office. Her reaction said it all. When she got home and opened the envelope Cheryl had given her, she was shocked by the contents.

"*Hannah please be careful. There have been rumours about strange things happening at the camp where Liz was working. She may have unwittingly upset some very powerful people. I'm not sure but Sam Lockwood may know something about this. Don't trust anyone. Even Simon Dresdon. Cheryl.*"

Hannah felt a complete whimp. In comparison to such a courageous friend as Liz, Hannah felt she useless.

"I imagine," Celia said breaking into her thoughts, "that my daughter was giving back something to society. She was trying to make a difference. It takes a very special person to do that. And my daughter was very special."

Well, that's put me in my place, thought Hannah. She smiled at Celia.

"We're thinking – that is I am thinking about Mary's suggestion – of establishing some sort of bursary to a charitable institute to commemorate her life."

"That's a wonderful idea, Celia." Hannah looked down at the box she was opening. "But why did you ask if Liz and I had fallen out over something?"

"Oh nothing really. But she made some disparaging comments about Paul in something I read and I wondered if she'd repeated them to you?"

"She was never one of Paul's fans. Although I did think they'd warmed to each other a little before he disappeared off the scene. He was at the funeral."

"Yes, I spoke to him. Charm personified. How did you feel about seeing him again?"

"Actually he'd already been to see me. He's threatening to take me to court so that he could have access to Elizabeth."

Celia said nothing but gave Hannah what seemed to be a pitying look.

TWENTY-SEVEN

"I don't know how you do it." Rory placed his pint and Hannah's large white wine on the table which wobbled in protest. None of the empties had been removed although the pub wasn't that busy – yet. It would soon be heaving with lunchtime drinkers.

"Do what exactly?" Hannah sipped her wine.

"Well you're not exactly investigative journalist of the year, are you?"

"And your point is?" She smiled to soften her reply but she had a feeling she knew what he was about to say and let him stew.

"What I mean is, you're not a hard-bitten hack – you're a good, competent woman's magazine writer who somehow manages to stumble on major stories."

Rory took a long gulp of beer, fascinated by Hannah's expression. At the moment she'd make a bloody awful poker player. Yet he knew there had to be another, almost ruthless streak beneath that soft-looking exterior. Judy with all her brittle nastiness would be no match for her, if Hannah decided to crush her. He wondered why she hadn't already. Perhaps she wasn't aware of this side of herself – yet.

Hannah placed her wine glass onto a wet patch on the tabled and pushed it round in a circle.

"It may surprise you to know that I would much rather have avoided discovering a dear friend murdered and as for…"

"Hannah I didn't mean… Look I'm sorry, that came out all wrong."

"Be careful if you're friends with me you might disappear or worse." For a moment Hannah looked as though she were about to cry. But she blinked rapidly and drank some more wine.

"So where are you up to and how can I help." Rory's businesslike tone restored a modicum of harmony.

Hannah didn't answer the question but fielded another. "How come some people are so evil? They can't be born that way…"

"Herd instinct I suppose. Once anyone starts some sort of scam…" Hannah's face now betrayed her indignation – "I mean crime – even if you're on the periphery it's difficult to extricate yourself without… oh I don't know. There's just a lot of complete bastards in the world. And sometimes no justice."

"Well could you imagine yourself getting caught up in something like this?"

"Hell no! But then I wouldn't be volunteering. I'm no do-gooder."

"Nor am I and I must say I was surprised that Liz was."

"So why do you think she went?"

"To get away from me." The words were out before she realised she had articulated her worst fear. "I think she went to get away from me."

"Bit extreme isn't it? Were you such a powerful influence on her?" Rory glanced at her over his pint. She looked fragile again and was blinking hard. "Sorry I didn't mean to upset you. But friends don't usually have such a profound effect."

"I was pregnant. I suppose I changed and I could see she was really pissed off with me at times going on about having a baby and…"

"Even so… there must be more to it."

"She had one of those foster children. You know the ones you sponsor…"

"Ye-es?"

"I think it was a combination of being fed up with me and that girl. Something happened to make her want to visit her."

"Hm that makes a bit more sense. Extreme, but a bit more understandable."

Hannah nodded but said nothing.

"I think we need to do a bit of digging about this charity, don't you?"

"Yes I was hoping you'd suggest that." Hannah had given just enough information to whet his appetite without exposing what else she feared. She was more wary now. *The News* might have her on a contract but she hadn't sold her soul. Not completely.

"Thanks Rory. Do you need to run it by George?"

He shook his head as he drained his glass. "No need for that at this stage. Let's see what we come up with first."

Hannah felt the relief as a wave of lightness that rippled through her. That had been easier thank she had anticipated. She smiled. "Now can I get you another drink?"

Rory glanced at his watch. "Why not?"

An overpowering scent of fresia. Hannah woke with a start. Once more she had fallen asleep in the armchair in Elizabeth's room. It had become a ritual to check on her sleeping daughter, to sit and gaze as Elizabeth snuffled in her sleep, flung an arm out of her duvet or chuckled at some unimaginable dream. Hannah sat and stared in mute adoration. Inevitably she fell asleep.

In the small glow of the nightlight the room was utterly peaceful. Hannah stretched and inhaled deeply. Fresia. Hardly a fragrance to grace a winter's evening. She tensed then relaxed as a smile spread across her face. Fresia. Her favourite flower. From wherever it had emanated, it felt like a message. An endorsement. A peace that she hadn't felt for so many months now, embraced her as she stood up and went into her own bedroom. She fell into a deep sleep almost as soon as she closed her eyes.

She awoke to chuckles and a hushed conversation that seemed to be coming from Elizabeth's room. Totally disorientated she leaped out of bed, thrusting herself into her dressing gown and walked in on Janet dressing Elizabeth as she chattered away and the toddler replied with happy laughter and the odd word.

Hannah watched in silence for a few moments. Janet had been a good choice.

"Hello you two."

Two relaxed faces turned to her, one smiling, one beaming.

"You look a lot better," Janet said.

"Thank you. Sorry I overslept. I…"

"It's no problem, Hannah. I realised when I let myself in you must still be asleep and Elizabeth was quite happy chatting to herself in her cot." She did up the last button on Elizabeth's cardigan. "Now madame you are ready to face the day. You go to Mummy while I go and make some coffee."

"Thank you," Hannah mouthed as she held her daughter close to her and breathed in her baby scent. No fresia this morning. Whatever it was in the night it had certainly helped her to sleep and feel more like facing life. Which was just as well as she had a long day ahead.

TWENTY-EIGHT

Hannah sat back and rubbed her eyes. She had spent the last couple of hours going through the microfiches that threw up any reference to her search for the charity and Somalia. There was a pile of notes on the table. Everything she had read made Liz's trip to Somalia seem even more unfathomable. And yet there was something…

She only had a few facts to go on but one was the girl Liz had "adopted". Liz had sent regular contributions for some time and received updates. Then they stopped. Both the payments and the communication. Why? Hannah had seen photos of the girl. She looked like an engaging child with a broad smile and a lively intelligent face. But then something had happened and there was a sadness reflected in her eyes. For want of a better word Hannah thought she looked as though she had been betrayed. But perhaps that was a flight of fancy. There were no further photos after that. So why did the payments stop? Hannah saw that it wasn't long afterwards that Liz had made her decision to volunteer for the charity.

Somalia couldn't have been an easy or comfortable place to be in. Frequent wars and uprisings led to an unstable and unsettled society. A society in which women had little say. It seemed the only thing the women were strong on was to perpetuate the mutilation of female genitalia. Hannah felt sick. Girls as young as six would be held down and cut and sewn like a piece of meat. She could imagine the screams of pain. The tears. And she wondered if Kamaria's sad photo marked her mutilation. Her female castration. Hannah shuddered. It was incomprehensible that a mother would do that to her child. And why? How could other women be complicit in such an aggressive and unnecessary act?

Hannah read that in 1983 55.4 per cent of women surveyed in Baydhaba, Somalia reported abnormal menstruation. Women who had undergone FGM were twice as likely to die during childbirth and more likely to give birth to a stillborn baby or one with brain damage. There were so many other awful side effects. So why?

She decided to try ringing James to ask him if he had come up with any contacts who would talk to her about what was, it seemed, a widespread problem for African women. Luck was on her side and she managed to reach him. His reaction wasn't promising.

"I'm still not sure about this, Hannah. I do know someone who could help you and she'd probably agree but…"

"But? Don't you trust me?"

"It's not you I don't trust, Hannah. But if you write anything for *The News* I'm not sure they wouldn't just sensationalise it and maybe undermine all the good work that is being done."

"First off I'm not even sure *The News* would carry any such story but I would have to offer it to them first. Secondly please give me some credit for handling this with integrity."

"Okay. I'll see what I can arrange and I'll be in touch."

Was their friendship now on the line? James obviously didn't trust her and if that was the case... His loss didn't bear thinking about.

Her research on the charity threw up very little. It was a minor player linked to other philanthropic bodies under umbrella organisations. Hannah wondered yet again why Liz had chosen such small time charity when she could presumably have had her pick of those in the major league like the Red Cross and Médecin Sans Frontiers. None of it made sense. Unless WelcAf really was the only charity which worked in the area that Liz's adopted child lived in.

News on the microfiche was sparse. However Rory had a contact in the Foreign Office and he was going to try that source.

Just as she was leaving the library her mobile rang.

"Hannah, it's Jane. I've just got back from Berlin and heard about what happened to Liz. You must be gutted. Can we meet up and talk?"

Hannah felt a warm glow inside her. Jane hadn't known Liz very well but she would understand Hannah's grief.

"Of course it will be so good to see you. Could you come to me so I don't have to get a babysitter? I'll cook supper."

"Ok but we'll get a take away – my treat. Are you free tomorrow evening?"

Hannah didn't like to say she was free most evenings. It sounded so lame and needy even if true. "Yes – will Chris be coming with you?"

"No he had to stay on for work. So just the two of us, wine, food and talk."

"You don't know how good that sounds." Hannah was enveloped in a sense of peace. Jane was back. Jane would help her put what had happened into some perspective.

Meantime there was someone else who could help with perspective. Hannah decided to broach Claudia Turner. She hadn's heard any updates for a while now and could use this excuse to sound out the inspector. On the third call she managed to reach her. "What happened to Jacob Gurnstein?" she asked with no preamble.

"What do you mean what happened to him?" Claudia's tone told her she wasn't going to get very far here but Hannah persisted.

"I suppose the obvious question is, did he jump or was he pushed?"

"His death is still part of an ongoing investigation, Hannah. Nothing salacious as yet for *The News* to get its teeth into."

"Well, I wasn't actually asking on behalf of *The News*. I'm sure Father Patrick, had he been able, would have organised a funeral for instance… he must have had one by now." Hannah couldn't mention that she'd been tipped off by Lucy. The less DI Claudia Turner knew about her own "investigations" the better.

"He did. His family saw to that."

"Family?"

"Yes they recognsied him from the photo and we released the body to them. They didn't want any fuss or publicity. So we honoured their wishes and withheld the information."

"I see." Convenient, Hannah thought and wondered about this family. "Do you think they'd talk to me as part of my follow up article on Liz?"

"I wouldn't think so." Claudia was dismissive. "They're a very private family with no wish to expose their relative or themselves to press scrutiny."

"Well if you hear that they've changed their minds, perhaps you'll give them my number?"

Claudia Turner's silence told Hannah all she needed to know – the DI would not pass on her details. Instead she asked, "Tell me, Hannah, I'm curious. Why would you think there's any connection – apart from the obvious one of his attending Liz Rayman's surgery – between his death and Liz's?"

"Just exploring ideas really. Seemed a strange coincidence, that's all. Plus there's Father Patrick…"

"Yes, Father Patrick. Look I have to go now. Keep in touch."

Hannah knew she was being fobbed off but there was little if anything she could do about it.

TWENTY-NINE

"Paul? Paul turned up here? Well that just takes the biscuit. The bastard! What did he think – that you'd fall at his feet grateful for any crumbs from his table?"

Hannah laughed. Jane and her indignation was just the tonic she needed. They'd ordered an Indian takeaway to be delivered and it was now spread before them on the coffee table and they had nearly finished the first bottle of wine.

"That's not the best of it." Hannah helped herself to some more green chicken handi and rice. "He's also seeing Judy Burton at *The News.*" Hannah managed to impart this piece of gossip with an equanimity she was far from feeling.

"Nooooo!" Jane had a forkful of food halfway to her mouth and and looked like some sort of cartoon character betraying her incredulity. "He told you that?"

"No I discovered it at the office when I was there. Someone was going on about Judy's latest prey and his name came up."

"So how did you feel about that?"

"To be honest it was like a physical blow. I nearly passed out.

Judy's a vicious cow but I don't think she knew of my connection to Paul. I'm sure if she had known she'd have made me aware of it. If Rory hadn't been there to push me onto a chair I think I'd have completely disgraced myself. He was a real Samaritan and took me for a drink and a sandwich."

"Did you tell him?" Jane had known Paul casually but had no time for him once he and Hannah had split up. But she had a lot of time for Rory whom she'd worked with.

"No I said that I hadn't eaten and it was low blood sugar."

"Well if he believed that, he's not much of a hack…"

"I don't think he did believe me but he was too much of a gentleman to push the point. And he's being really supportive with helping me look into Liz's murder."

Jane's expression was deadpan. She had worked on *The News* as the chief sub and had in fact got Hannah her first commission there. "So how exactly has this come about. Doesn't sound like *The News* to let you loose on a major news story. No offence," she said quickly seeing the look of indignation on Hannah's face.

"None taken and you're right, *The News* is only letting me write first person accounts of what it's like to lose a friend like this etc etc." Hannah made a face. "You needn't worry they haven't gone soft on me and Judy is champing at the bit and after my blood. God knows what she'd be like if she knew about the Paul connection."

"Hmmm I wonder…"

"Wonder what?"

"Just a thought that's going round in my mind. I'll let you know if it bears fruit. So you still haven't explained how …"

"Lady Rayman, Liz's mother…"

"I know who Lady Rayman is."

"Well she asked me to investigate for her. A bit like a private detective, I suppose and she's paying me. I wasn't happy about accepting her suggestion – or money – but she has a way of getting people to do her bidding. I assume she thinks that as a friend, I'll be kind to Liz's memory if anything untoward emerges."

"And has it?"

"Not really. She was pregnant when she died and…"

"Shit – did you know she was having a baby?"

"No. I think she was going to tell me on the night she died. At least I assume she was. What's that look for?"

"What look? You just sound … oh I don't know. Take no notice of me. Who was the father?"

"That's what's so odd, there's no clue as to who the father was. I didn't even know she was seeing someone. Lady Rayman didn't know either. The pregnancy was mentioned in the post mortem report." Hannah shocked herself at how dispassionately she could talk about Liz – now in the past tense.

Jane finished her wine. "What a bloody awful time you've been having."

"Well it's not just me. There's the odd connection with the vicar at St John's where Liz held her weekly surgery. He…" Hannah was about to mention the blackmail when she thought better of it. "He's currently in St Thomas's and –"

"Curiouser and curiouser. Shall we open another bottle?"

Hannah smiled. "Some things never change. It's so good to have you back in London Jane."

"Sounds as though I've come at the right time."

With their glasses replenished, they smiled at one another. Each wondering how much they could or should actually say.

Something restrained Hannah. She'd known Jane forever but there was always a but these days. Last year she had wondered how much Chris had actually known about Gerry Lacon when he'd accused him of buying kidneys from improverished immigrants for transplants. A claim Lacon hadn't denied. That question left her feeling more vulnerable than she'd care to admit.

"So how's Tom faring in the States?" Jane's words broke into Hannah's thoughts. "How long is he away for?"

"Think the answer to both those questions is that I don't know. And if you're going to ask about him and me the answer's the same."

"Oh Hannah –" Jane leaned over to envelope her in a hug. "Nothing's ever simple in your life is it?"

"So who needs simple." Hannah swallowed the anguish rising in her throat and raised her glass. "To complicated friends." She smiled and wondered what sort of complications Jane might have in her life just now. Especially as Chris hadn't returned to London with her.

THIRTY

When is not telling the truth an outright lie? Hannah had been a journalist long enough to know how you sometimes had to manipulate the truth for a good story. She tried to maintain her intergrity but you could never control the way the subs attacked your story or the headlines they used. It was her let-out clause when interviewing. Her folow-up article including the interview with Michael Dresdon was a case in point. Although she'd tried to show the charity in a positive light, mentioning low resources but honorable commitment, someone else had dug up some dirt and added it to the article. In a not so suble way, the article now implied that the charity was remiss in the way it sent workers out to a country which was effectively in the midst of a civil war or at least one prey to ever more frequent terrorist attacks.

"While we applaud the philanthropic motives of our countrymen and women, should we encourage them to work in war zones, putting their lives and maybe the lives of others at risk" was not in her original copy.

Nor was "maybe these charity workers are naïve and too trusting or perhaps have an inflated sense of their own capabilities? Who knows?" Who indeed. Certainly not desk-bound subs, that's for sure.

Hannah threw the newspaper onto the floor. She was coming up against dead ends all the way. She was no nearer finding out who had killed or had arranged to have Liz killed which seemed a more likely scenario. The Cardboard City dwellers were an easy target for the press in general. They were an amorphous group. People came and went. Some died as Jacob Gurnstein had. In death, at least, he had been reunited with his family. She wondered who he really was. Everything on the police front seemed to have gone quiet. A cold case before it was ever a case. Another silent judgement. But by whom?

Hannah remembered his voice as he had called out to her on the night of Liz's murder. And his face on the photograph Liz had had. There was something commanding about him. Idly she wondered what had led him to leave his family and friends and live as he had done. The journalist in her would have loved to write his story…

THIRTY-ONE

What infuriated Hannah was that there was nothing she could do to help Father Patrick. Although the police – mainly DI Turner – thought she would be useful to him, Hannah was only too aware that this was no two-way street. DI Turner had given her minimal information and there was no way she could even enter his home, let alone search it.

Almost reiterating the threat from the bishop who had conducted Liz's funeral, the archdeacon had made it perfectly clear to her that the church resented her intrusion as they saw it into matters that were no concern of hers when he had invited her to his office.

His invitation had been phrased in terms that made it seem like an offer she couldn't refuse when he had telephoned her. Hannah had thought about refusing or at least on insisting the meeting was at a place of her choosing. But where? She certainly didn't want him in her home. However she was curious as to what they might know about Patrick's situation.

"They're political animals these archdeacons," Reverend

Daniels had told Hannah when she phoned him for advice. "They concentrate on canonical law and overseeing the clergy.

"The best thing is to say as little as possible. Use your journalistic skills. They will protect Father Patrick if they can – if not they might throw him to the wolves."

Hannah was surprised by the office they met in. The Venerable Andrew Fawshore's invitation may have been more like a royal command, but where he conducted his business was far from palatial. The room was small and, as one would imagine, lined with books on two walls. The third was covered with religious icons and a huge wooden cross. The fourth wall, behind the desk, had a window that appeared to look out on only the backs of buildings, and was covered with a venetian blind with the slats angled away from the view.

"So Miss Weybridge…" He was a thin man, dressed in black apart from his clerical collar. His hair matched his clothes and was neatly parted to one side. There seemed little joy in him. But if John Daniel's was right, perhaps dealing with the miscreants might had drained that from him.

"It's Ms Weybridge."

"Ms." The archdeacon's monobrow rose. "Indeed Ms Weybridge. First let me offer my sincere condolences about the loss of your friend. Most unfortunate."

He made it seem as though Liz's death was an inconvenience. That somehow she had brought it upon herself and had the temerity to meet her murderer in one of the churches he was responsible for. Hannah cursed him silently but kept what she hoped was a neutral expression on her face and said nothing.

"I don't know how much you are aware of the arrangements between Father Patrick and Miss – Ms – Rayman. The rooms below St John's are used by a number of organisations – some from

Lambeth Council – to help those in need. We have social workers, mental health workers…"

"And a dentist." Hannah finished the list for him.

"Quite."

"And she was there at Father Patrick's request." The archdeacon's monobrow made an upward journey again. "She met him at a charity fundraiser." Hannah wanted to distance Liz's contribution from the others who were paid to work there. "She gave her services for free and wasn't part of any council initiative."

The archdeacon's double chin – incongruous with his thin frame – wobbled slightly as he swallowed this information. Clearly he wasn't used to being questioned or interrupted. His eyes behind a pair of wire-framed glasses narrowed slightly.

"Do you think they had a close relationship?" He leaned back in the chair in a way that made his torso concave, like a snake.

"I have no idea," Hannah could answer this question truthfully. "When I found Liz it was the first time I had been to St John's and I'd only heard her mention Father Patrick in passing, as the one who had inveighled her into running her surgery there."

"Why do you say 'inveighled'?" the archdeacon's smile betrayed his condescension.

"Well I can't think it was her idea. She has – had – a private practice in the Barbican for a start."

"But had not long returned from volunteering overseas, Somalia, I think." He let that thought rest. That was common knowledge and had been included in her own article for *The News*.

"Archdeacon, you invited me here to talk about Father Patrick, I assume. I really can't help you. If you think there's a link between Liz's murder and his assault…"

The eyebrow did its thing again. "An interesting choice of word."

"What would you call it then?"

The archdeacon spread his hands. "I only know what the police have chosen to tell me. As yet I haven't been permitted to see Father Patrick." The question "have you?" was implicit but Hannah answered with a question of her own.

"What were the police looking for in the church?"

The archdeacon shrugged. "Your guess is as good as mine. I suppose it was connected to your friend's murder."

"But they were turning the vicarage upside down as well. I heard they'd even been digging up the garden." Once again she saw the leering face of that horrid sergeant as she'd walked past.

"A complete waste of police time and resources, I think. Father Patrick may have been misguided in his choice of company but I cannot image for one moment that he has any real skeletons buried under his patio. Anyway from what I understand from the police it was a tip-off from a member of the public. Probably a malicious member of the congregation whom he upset in some way."

Hannah bristled at the reference to "his choice of company". Is that how the church viewed Liz. An unfortunate choice? For Patrick maybe and maybe not. She wondered how much the archdeacon knew about this malicious person. Was he – or she – the same one who was blackmailing him? And then she remembered what Patrick had told her, that just before Liz was murdered he'd been called out to the hospital – on a wild goose chase as it happened.

"Does that happen often, then?" she asked.

"Does what happen often?"

"Members of a church congregation casting aspersions on their vicar out of pure malice?"

"More often than you'd think, I suspect," the archdeacon replied. "But I wonder at your role in all this is, Ms Weybridge? Why are you so involved?"

"Liz was my friend…"

"Yes but not Father Patrick as far as I am aware?"

Hannah wondered just how much he was aware of. "No we only met after Liz's death." Hannah decided to play a wild card. "Did you know he'd been called away from St John's to the hospital just before Liz's murder. That's why she was alone in the church."

"That's not unusual if a member of the congregation has asked for their vicar…"

"Yes but when he arrived there was no parishioner. No one had asked for him. By the time he got back it was too late." Hannah could hear the frustated anger in her own voice.

"No I didn't know that. I assume Father Patrick told you that?"

Hannah nodded. "Rather casts a different light on the tip-off to the police as well, doesn't it?"

The archdeacon made a note on a pad he had with him. "Yes and no. But this is a matter for the diocese and the police, Ms Weybridge. Not for some salacious story in *The News*."

"I am also acting for Lady Rayman who obviously wants to find out why her daughter died that night. Anyway you can't stop me writing about whatever I uncover."

"Mm have to check that out with our legal department… However I would advise you to act with caution. Sometimes it's best to let sleeping dogs lie."

"Or even comatose priests?" Hannah couldn't resist the jibe. She couldn't see that anything else could be gained from continuing the conversation. She looked at her watch. "I'm sorry but I have another meeting…"

"And I have been remiss, taking up your time and not even offering you some refreshment… Thank you for coming, Ms Weybridge. I hope your friend's murder will be solved soon."

"So do I."

Hannah shook his outstretched hand as he said, "Peace be with you," then left.

She hadn't told him everything. Especially not the fact that Patrick had said he was being blackmailed. Let them find that out for themselves. Little good it would do them, she thought. Pompous prig!

She wondered not for the first time if Patrick was the father of Liz's child. Surely he wasn't being blackmailed for that? Still a man of God having a child "out of wedlock". It had been bad enough for her. So many people pitied her or told her in no uncertain terms what they thought of single mothers sponging on the state. They ignored the fact that she had her own home and supported herself financially. The government blamed everything on single mothers rarely acknowleding how many women had had to bring up children on their own after two wars – and made a good job of it.

She thought of Elizabeth and felt a warmth suffuse her body. Worth every ounce of disapproval. Then the image of Paul intruded on her joy. What the hell was he playing at? Had he made the connection between Judy and her? That he was deliberately seeing the staff journalist to get at her seemed too far-fetched. *Coincidences do happen*, she thought, as she made her way down to Borough High Street.

THIRTY-TWO

Coincidences. Life was full of them. But most of them were insignificant. Hannah didn't think the assault on Father Patrick was connected to Liz's murder. On the other hand, it might have been to do with what he was being blackmailed about. But it seemed more than a coincidence that he had been called away from St John's so that Liz had been there on her own.

Hannah took a taxi to *The News* offices and went to the cuttings library. She'd decided to run a search on Father Patrick, Church of England politics and anything else that this led her to. She'd never thought about Patrick's sexuality but supposing he had nothing to do with Liz's pregnancy? What if he was gay and had been caught out? She thought of her friend Joe Rawlington and how careful he was. Joe had no reason to hide his homosexuality but to all intents and purposes he did.

Being gay had been decriminalised for over twenty-five years. But still, her researches revealed, gays and bisexuals were convicted for acts that would not have been a crime with a woman. The figures were sickening. In 1989, during the Conservative campaign for family values, more than 2,000 men were prosecuted for gross indecency, as many as during the 1950s and nearly three times the numbers in the mid-sixties.

But still Hannah couldn't understand Joe. After all the MP Chris Smith had come out ten years ago… If Joe was reticent, how much more difficult for a member of the clergy. The church of England seemed uncompromising in their "homosexuality is a sin" stance. Plus the age of consent for homosexuals was twenty-one.

Perhaps Father Patrick had had a liaison with someone younger than twenty-one? It was all pure speculation and likely to remain so. She couldn't see the archdeacon being willing to discuss this with her and poor Patrick was in no fit state.

Why else would he have been blackmailed? Hannah wondered what the blackmailer would do now? Had he – or she – been responsible for what had happened to Patrick? But that didn't make sense. If he'd died he certainly wouldn't have been able to pay up. So if not the blackmailer then who?

Hannah felt gripped by a cold terror which chilled her to the bone. Surely people in the church would not do such a thing? But what if it were linked to Liz? Had she told Patrick something that he would be able to use against the people behind whatever was going on in that village in Somalia? Maybe the blackmail was a ruse and when that didn't work…

Father Patrick's name came up in none of the searches she'd tried. She'd even tried "gay priests". Several names – surprisingly more that she would have thought – came up. Evidently some were prepared to stand up and be counted. She wondered how that would affect their careers. Did one have a career structure in the church? Archdeacon to bishop or were there other avenues they could pursue? Well Patrick wouldn't be doing much pursuing now, she supposed.

Hannah's mind was going round in circles. She needed a break. And she knew just the thing.

Hannah made her way carefully down the stairs into the gloom of the City Golf Club, near St Brides, the journalists' church off Fleet Street. It was busy with afternoon drinkers as it most often was. Joe was sitting in a corner and waved. He already had a bottle of white and two glasses on the table. He stood up and kissed her. "This is a lovely surprise – thought you didn't emerge during daylight hours these days."

Hannah laughed. "Or night time if the truth be told. But I was over at *The News* and I suddenly thought I hadn't seen you in ages and I could do with some friendly company."

"As bad as that eh?" He poured the wine. Running his own PR company meant his hours were never fixed and he often worked evenings and weekends so Hannah knew he felt justified in taking a late lunch now and again and had rung to see if he were free.

"Well put it this way, I met an archdeacon today who makes Cruella look like an an animal lover. I never realised Christians could be so grim. Did you see that bishop at the funeral?"

"I'd have been hard put not to, he did conduct the service. What about him?"

"He told me not to meddle in things and he… seemed to know a lot about me."

"Maybe he had asked Lady Rayman about you. He may have just been interested in who was going to speak during the service."

"Perhaps." Hannah look a long gulp of wine. "But there was something in the way he spoke to me. I felt I was being threatened."

Joe was quiet for a moment. "You don't think you're reading too much into it? Remember you're still raw from that girl Caroline's death."

Why does everyone call her "that girl"? Hannah wondered not for the first time. She had promised herself she was not going to be defined by what happened last year.

"I'm trying to put all that behind me." Hannah smiled. "Anyway how are *you*?"

"Fine. Well, more than fine, actually. I'm thinking of standing for the local council. There's a by-election as someone resigned." A long time member of the Labour party, Jack had previously resisted all invitations to stand for office.

"I think that's a great idea. What made you change your mind? You were always so adamant about not standing."

Joe actually looked bashful – amazing for a hardened PR man. "I've met someone. And I think it's time to stand up and be counted."

Hannah raised her glass. "I'll drink to that. When am I going to meet him? He must be very special."

"He is – and all in good time. He's helping me with my election campaign. It's a safe seat and …

"And you can get a bit of experience before the next general election." Hannah winked at him.

"Yes, that's the idea."

Hannah hugged him. "I'm so glad. You'll make a brilliant MP. As long as you don't have any skeletons rattling around in your cupboards."

"Not that I know of." Joe smiled. "Have you?"

"That would be telling." She paused before going on, "But seriously what would you do, if there were?"

Joe contemplated the question while he poured more wine. "I suppose that would depend on how long the skeleton and been there and who else might be affected. Where's this leading, Hannah?"

Hannah took a deep breath and crossed her fingers under the table. "A friend of mine is being blackmailed."

"And?"

"And he asked for my help…"

"Because you're an expert in dealing with blackmailers?" Joe snorted so loudly, some of the other drinkers looked their way.

"I think he might be gay."

"That's not a crime unless…"

"Unless the other person was under twenty-one."

"Exactly. Seems you'd be better off asking him a few questions rather than me. How's that beautiful daughter of yours."

Hannah took the hint as Joe changed the subject. "Practically perfect like me." She refilled their glasses.

"By the way, remember Jane and Chris?"

"How could I forget them after that dinner last year?" Joe had been at there when Chris had tormented Jane Lacon about her political allegiances and castigated her husband for running a clinic that bought kidneys from improverished immigrants for transplants for his rich private patients. The couple had left mid-meal.

"Indeed. Chris can come on a bit strong." She had never told Joe about Gerry Lacon's involvement with Caroline's death or that he'd had been going shoot her baby. "Anyway Jane is back from Berlin but he's still there."

"But they haven't broken up?"

"I don't think so. Jane said something about his contract being extended but she needed to be back in London for an assignment."

"In any event it must be nice for you to have Jane around."

"It will be – and I've missed you too."

"I haven't been away." Joe smiled and placed his well manicured hand over hers.

"I know but I have – metaphorically speaking."

"Then let's drink to your return. Shall we have another glass – if you have time?"

Hannah looked at her watch. "I have – let's go for it."

For a short time life seemed to be as it had once been – without the shadow of death and uncertainty. Hannah realised afterwards that Joe had never once mentioned Tom.

THIRTY-THREE

Hannah was looking at the prints of the photos she'd taken in the Bull Ring. Even with some enhancement, most of them were too dark. Shame someone hasn't invented a hidden flash as well, she thought.

The telephone rang. She was tempted to let it ring through to answerphone but so many people hated leaving messages. At least the people she'd most like to hear from did.

She reached over and picked up the handset. "Hannah Weybridge."

"Good morning. This is Simon Ryan." There was a pause. "Patrick Ryan's brother."

"Oh hello." It had never occurred to Hannah that Patrick might have a sibling. She'd assumed that because no one had turned up at the hospital, and Claudia Turner hadn't mentioned them, that he didn't have any close relatives. Erroneous assumption as it now transpired.

"I just found your card among Patrick's things so..." he let the sentence tail off.

That's the second card of mine he had, thought Hannah who was sure she'd hadn't given him one at all. Why would she? He'd already had her telephone number from Lady Rayman she assumed when he had told her that Lady Rayman had recommended her to him. However Liz may have given him her cards – perhaps she had been worried about her safety even when she was back in the UK.

"Where are you? Have you been to see Patrick?"

"I have and I'm at the vicarage now."

"Oh have the police finished there then?" Silly question – of course they had.

"Yes. Look I'd rather not have this conversation over the phone. Would you meet me here? There are some things I'd like to ask you and it'd be much better face to face."

Simon Ryan looked just like an older version of his brother but with more assurance. He wore a dark suit that looked bespoke and his hair was flecked with a few strands of grey. He was an imposing figure who looked as though he was used to getting what he wanted. Hannah smiled. How unalike could two brothers be?

"Good to meet you, Hannah and thanks for taking the time to come here."

"I don't know Patrick very well at all," she said. "It was my friend Liz who knew him."

Simon picked up on the past tense. "Yes of course, your friend who was murdered in the church. You found her didn't you? That must have been a terrible shock. Please – sit down."

They were in Patrick's study cum sitting room. The room he had brought her to. It didn't look any different although the police must have been through everything in their searches.

"Would you like some tea, or coffee?"

"No thank you. This is all a bit of a surprise. I'd assumed Patrick didn't have any close relatives or wasn't in touch with his family."

She watched Simon's face reflect his sadness as he explained, "Our parents are elderly – our father has Parkinsons which means my mother is more or less his carer and has little time for anything or anyone else." That was said in a matter of fact way that Hannah couldn't help feeling covered the hurt he was feeling. "I was involved in a major case and couldn't get here any sooner. I'm a barrister," he said to Hannah's unspoken question.

"Well it must have come as shock to you to hear about your bother like that."

"Yes, it was. I was rather hoping you might throw some light on the situation for me." He smiled. "Are you sure I can't tempt you to some coffee? I'm going to have one."

Hannah accepted and followed him into the kitchen. It was a narrow galley type that led off from a dining room which looked more functional than decorative. The kitchen was well organised as though thought had gone into making everything easy to get to with the minimum of effort. Simon seemed to know where everything was.

"Have you been here often?" Hannah asked as he poured boiling water into the coffee pot.

"Odd question. We're brothers. I usually visit between cases. Only for a couple of nights or so. Patrick always spends his holidays with our parents. Gives Mum a break – and me." He smiled and Hannah saw again the likeness between the brothers.

"Let's take this through, shall we?" He picked up the tray of coffee and a plate of biscuits. "Patrick always keeps a good supply of tea, coffee and biscuits for his parishioners. Not sure he bothers quite so much about his own proper meals though." He sighed. Hannah thought he looked the type of man who ate – and drank – well.

"Now, tell me. What do you know of my brother's predicament?"

Hannah accepted the coffee he handed to her. "Very little. You probably know more than I do as I'm sure you've been in contact with the police."

"Yes a DI Turner spoke to me. After they'd sent a local officer to see my parents. Mum rang me immediately, of course, and I made some enquiries. But as I said I was in the middle of a major case which then suddenly collapsed, so here I am." He sipped his coffee.

"It would seem Patrick owes his life to one of the down and outs who come to the church." He looked solemn. "God knows what would have happened if he hadn't acted so swiftly."

"A guardian angel." Hannah spoke the words before she realised she's said them aloud.

"Quite." Simon waited.

Hannah put down her cup. "Your brother rang me and asked me to meet him in the church. As you can imagine it wasn't a place I wanted to return to but Patrick said he had something to show me. It was a ruse. He wanted me to see that the beauty and sacredness remained unsullied. Then we came here and he told me. that he was being blackmailed and wanted my help."

Simon nodded but said nothing. Hannah wondered why he didn't ask why Patrick had contacted her. It occurred to her that he'd already made enquiries about her and knew far more than he was saying.

"Did he say why he was being blackmailed?"

"No he didn't and when I suggested that someone in the church hierarchy would be better placed to advise him, he was adamant that he couldn't go to them. Having met the archdeacon I can see why…"

"Full of his own importance, isn't he. Still, I suppose he means well." Simon didn't sound convinced.

"If I'd known he has a brother who's a barrister I'd have told him to contact you. Is it strange that he didn't?"

Simon Ryan said nothing for a moment and drank his coffee. "Maybe he had his reasons."

"I did wonder if he was the father of Liz's unborn child…"

Simon nearly choked on his coffee. "Hannah my brother is gay, he's far more likely to have been blackmailed about that, but as far as I know he is celibate."

Hannah shrugged. There were ways and means. Just because he was gay didn't mean he couldn't father a child. But she kept that thought to herself. "Then I wonder if Liz had told him about her time in Somalia? She said very little to me when she returned earlier than expected. But I think things were happening there which had a profound effect on her."

Hannah was going to say more then thought the better of it. It could be that he'd find out more if she didn't put ideas into his head.

"Well that's something to work on, isn't it." He wrote down the name of the charity and their contact details.

"How long are you staying for?"

"As long as I need to." He looked at his watch. "Visiting time. I'd like to keep in touch if that's ok with you? Maybe we can help each other."

Hannah smiled. "Yes do you have a mobile number or should I leave a message on the vicarage answerphone?"

"No don't leave a message here, contact me directly." He handed her a card as she stood to leave. "Nice to meet you even if under such sad cirmcumstances."

As Hannah left she felt it was unlikely she'd get to see Patrick again now that his brother was here. He looked a good match for DI Turner.

THIRTY-FOUR

They were sitting side by side in her sitting room. James and the most beautiful black woman she had ever encountered. Tall and slim she had an aristocratic bearing and seemed to glide rather than walk. Her hair was cropped short and her smile was hesitant. James clasped her hand. "This is my cousin, Mia. Mia's family comes from Somalia and she can tell you what you need to know."

He stood up.

"Aren't you staying?" Hannah felt slightly panicky.

"No. It will be better if you talk together without me. I'll come back later. Don't get up, I know where the front door is." He smiled at Mia and nodded to Hannah.

Both women where silent until they heard the front door close.

"May I offer you something to drink Mia? Tea, coffee… a glass of wine?" she added hopefully.

"No I'm fine thank you. Perhaps when James returns..?" Mia's deep brown eyes betrayed both sadness and hope making Hannah wonder at their relationship.

"Of course. It's very good of you to take the time to talk to me.

You do know I am a journalist?"

"Yes that is why I agreed to come here. I thought you might be able to write about this in some way to highlight the problem we have."

"The problem?"

"Yes in my birth country they carry out female circumcision." She paused looking embarassed but she didn't look away. In fact she seemed to stare at Hannah more keenly almost daring her to comment.

"Do you mind if I take notes while you are talking, Mia. Or perhaps recording our conversation?" Hannah added this with little hope of an agreement so was taken aback by Mia's reaction.

"Of course, record it. You will be able to concentrate better on what I am going to tell you."

Hannah stood up. "Excuse me I just get my dictaphone." She dashed upstairs and returned within a couple of minutes. Mia looked as though she hadn't moved a muscle.

Hannah sat down and switched on the machine. Without prompting, Mia began her story.

"As I said in my country they carry out female cricumcision – Female Genital Mutilation. But no one talks about it in that way. Young girls, children really, are tricked into believing they are going to a special celebration. I remember, when it happened to me, feeling very excited. We were visiting my grandparents and were told there was going to be a big party. A whole group of us – there must have been eleven or twelve children – were led into a separate room. There was lots of music – drumming – I could hear. Little did I know why." Mia stopped talking. She looked absolutely terrified. "I'm sorry Hannah, do you think I could have a glass of water? Actually a glass of wine would be better."

Hannah nodded and returned with wine and two glasses plus a jug of water and tumblers on a tray. She poured the wine. They both took large gulps. Then Mia laughed. "I shouldn't need Dutch courage, but I do."

Hannah raised her glass in salute and turned on the tape recorder again.

"One by one we were led into another room. When it was my turn, the atmosphere in that room was very different. I was grabbed by each arm and a piece of cloth was tied over my eyes. I fought but there were so many of them. I was wrestled to the floor and what must have been a very large woman sat on my chest. I thought I was going to die from suffocation. Other women took my arms and pinned them down while my legs were spread apart."

Some more wine punctuated Mia's monologue.

"I want you to know this Hannah. I fought with everything I had in me. But I was just a small child. I screamed for all I was worth and the beating of the drums got louder and louder. And then there was the pain. I cannot describe this pain. It was unbearable. They stuffed some cloth in my mouth. I could feel the heat of the blood oozing from me. I thought I was going to die, I really did."

Hannah's tears cascaded down her face. Mia reached forward and clutched Hannah's hand. "I am a survivor. I am still fighting. I will not be a victim. I am using my experience to try to prevent this happening to others."

"What in the UK?"

"Yes in the UK. But also girls, like me, are taken back to their country of origin to be mutilated by this barbaric procedure. I am trying to educated families here. But also in my homeland."

Both women were silent. Hannah topped up their glasses. There was a click and a whirl as the cassette tape came to an end. Hannah switched off the machine.

Mia spoke first. "Hannah I am really glad you are going to write about this but I would prefer that my name is not mentioned. There are people who don't like what I am doing and I don't want to give them any more ammunition against me."

"Of course, Mia." She clutched her hand. "I don't think I've ever met anyone as courageous as you are."

By the time James returned they had started on another bottle of wine and he joined them. He looked as though he needed a drink more than Mia and she wondered yet again about their relationship. Cousins. But cousins marry. An arranged marriage? But that didn't seem likely. And anyway James's mother was British and...

They left not long afterwards and Hannah was left with the nightmare that had been Mia's early experiences echoing in her mind. Especially Mia's last words to her: "Hannah if your friend was killed because of something that happened in Somalia, I don't think it would be because of the cutting. I think it's much more likely to be about the kidnapping and raping of young girls by the terrorist forces."

Hannah stared at her as James gave her a quick peck on the cheek and they were gone.

After she'd cleared away downstairs, Hannah crept into her sleeping daughter's room and gazed down at her adored child and thought of Mia. How could any mother let that happen to a child they loved? Then she remembered that Mia had said the mothers weren't allowed to be present for just that reason. They wouldn't be able to listen to their daughters' screams and not try to protect them.

But Hannah also had something else to worry about. Had Liz tried to intervene against the terrorist forces. What had she done? What could she have done? Except break what might have been a conspiracy of silence within the charity? But surely the charity wouldn't have sanctioned Liz's murder. So who else would have had the motive and the wherewithall to arrange for Liz's execution – for that it what Liz's murder now seemed like?

THIRTY-FIVE

"Do you know anything about Simon Ryan, he's a barrister based in Manchester, I believe?"

Rory shrugged. "Name rings a bell but…"

"He's Father Patrick Ryan's brother." Hannah bit into her sandwich. Once again they were sitting in the pub opposite *The News*'s offices after what had been for Hannah a very short editorial meeting. She'd only been brought in at the end and had the distinct feeling she had been the subject of an earlier discussion.

"Is he now..?" Rory tapped on his glass. "From what I can remember he takes on high profile criminal trials. Defence barrister. We could see what the cuttings library can drag up." Rory took a long gulp of beer.

"You look as though you needed that." Hannah smiled.

"I did. This abduction case has wiped nearly everything off the news agenda."

Hannah shuddered. "What on earth was the mother doing letting go of the child's hand like that."

"Come on Hannah, be fair. She only turned away for a moment to pay the shop assistant."

"That's all it takes…"

"Christ you're bloody judgemental today. Have you never looked the other way, made a slip?"

Hannah's eyes welled up and her cheeks flushed. "I'm sorry I didn't mean to… You should write a piece on it. What it feels like for a mother to…"

"You must be joking." Hannah looked aghast.

"No I'm not. Use it Hannah. It could be cathartic. Also it would justify your retainer. Judy would never be able to do the story justice."

"You're serious aren't you? Did George put you up to this?"

Rory had the grace to look embarrassed. "She did mention it." Hannah had always wondered just how much Georgina Henderson knew about Gerry Lacon and his attack on her. They had never discussed it. After Hannah's story about him and his clinic had been spiked there had been a news blackout. Certainly his attack on her had never been made public. Hannah's stomach tightened. She was having her strings pulled yet again and it was not a pleasant feeling.

"Wish I'd never signed that bloody contract."

"Well you did so you'd better make the most of it. Come on Hannah you've got to play the game."

"And if I don't?" Even to her own ears Hannah sounded petulant.

"Why make life difficult for yourself? Want another?" He pointed to Hannah's almost empty wine glass.

"No thanks. Better get going."

"But you didn't finish your story. How did you meet Simon Ryan?"

"He contacted me. He's in London to be with his brother and

staying at the vicarage. Apparently he'd been tied up by some high profile case he'd been working on—"

"That'd be the Druffield case. A witness suddenly withdrew his evidence and the trial collapsed. Conveniently."

"Why d'you say that?"

"A lot of people had reason to be glad there was no conviction."

Hannah, none the wiser, finished her drink. Rory had gone to the bar and returned with two more drinks.

"I didn't..."

"I know this is medicinal. You're going to drink this and relax and I'm going to book a car to take you home. Deal?"

Hannah raised her glass in a salute. "Deal. Anyway going back to Simon Ryan... at least with him on the scene I won't feel responsible for his brother."

"Why should you?"

"Oh because... all sorts of reasons. His link to Liz, I suppose." She had never told Rory about the blackmail threat. In spite of what Rory thought, she was learning to play the game. She might not be able to write for other newspapers but that wouldn't stop her feeding another journalist any info she had. As long as she didn't take any payment for it she assumed she wouldn't be deemed to be breaking her contract. She could just let a few facts slip during a conversation or just point someone in the tight direction...

"So this is where you hold your briefing meetings, then." Judy Burton's syrupy tones interrupted Hannah's thoughts. As usual, Judy looked stylish and glamorous in her Donna Karen dress and jacket, making Hannah feel distinctly shabby in comparison.

Rory, ever the gentleman, stood up. "What can I get you, Judy?"

Hannah hoped she'd say she was meeting someone but the woman she'd least like to be with sat down next to her. "Red wine, as you're in the chair, Rory. Thank you."

Hannah watched her settle herself and take her cigarettes and lighter out of her bag. She certainly made the best of herself, Hannah had to concede. She was really rather pretty if you weren't at the receiving end of her barbed comments. Her highlighted hair always looked freshly washed and blow dried and there were never any tell-tale roots. Hannah imagined she must spend a fortune – just on her hair.

"So, how's life with you Hannah?" Judy made a performance of lighting her cigarette. "Any updates on your friend's murder?"

"You probably know more that I do." Hannah concentrated on her wine.

"I'd have thought your little inspector friend could have pulled a few strings for you."

Hannah looked at her blankly. She couldn't be refering to Claudia Turner.

"What's his name? Tom Jordan."

The smile Hannah commanded her face to wear almost covered her agitation. "He's in the US at the moment but I'm sure you know that Judy."

Judy exhaled a long shaft of smoke but away from Hannah. "Not really that interested to be honest. I was just making conversation." She studied her nails, painted a deep red and looking like a bird of prey's talons to Hannah. A bird of prey who'd just mauled its victim.

"Did you know I'm seeing Paul Montague?" When she looked up Hannah could see the look of defiance combined with what seemed to be an entreaty in her eyes.

"I had heard." Hannah sipped her wine.

"I had no idea… really Hannah I didn't…"

"Nothing to do with me who you or Paul see. He's nothing to me Judy."

"But he's…"

"Charming, good looking and amusing company." Hannah smiled. She would never give Judy the satisfaction of knowing her true thoughts. It crossed her mind that Paul had put her up to this.

Judy inhaled the smoke from her cigarette. "I think he may be using me… to get at you."

Hannah stared at her indisbelief. "But I haven't had anything to do with him for nearly two years." Never had she seen herself in the role of reassuring this woman who had made it her business to be so unpleasant to her. "I really don't think so, Judy. He probably just likes you for who you are." Hannah did not mention Paul turning up at her home or making a claim on his daughter. But just for once she did feel a bit sorry for Judy. She wasn't dense…

"Thanks Rory. I needed this," Judy said. "Cheers." Rory had also bought drinks for himself and Hannah. She was about to protest when he gave a little shake of his head towards Judy. Maybe he thought this was a useful bonding session.

"Don't worry, I've booked you a car, Hannah. It'll be ready when you are."

"Oh the hard life of a freelance, eh?" Hannah assumed this was another barbed comment but Judy's face actually looked friendly. Miracles, it seemed, did sometimes happen.

THIRTY-SIX

Much to Hannah's astonishment, *The News* published her story on FGM. As her contract dictated she offered anything she wrote to the newspaper first, and she had done so with little expectation of them using it. She even wondered if they'd take it but not publish. Another spiked story. She was wrong. Under the title of "The cruellest cut of all", Mia's experiences and Hannah's description of them were treated sympathetically and respectfully.

Rory told her that Georgina was emphatic that it should not be sensationalised. The story, she said, spoke for itself. Mia's identity had not been revealed in Hannah's copy and Georgina hadn't asked her for it.

Hannah was amazed and confessed as much to Rory when they were having lunch in the pub.

"George's not such a dragon you know. Anyway I don't think any woman – or any man come to that – could read that article and not be moved. It's horrendous, Hannah. Unimaginable for most of us. Well done you – you've done it again."

Hannah smiled. "Yeah I know, not bad for a woman's mag journo."

Rory raised his glass to her and look a long drink of beer. "So how's all the other investigating going?"

"Lots of dead ends, I'm afraid." Hannah was wary of what she revealed. She liked Rory and he was being supportive but – there was always a but. "Liz had to be murdered for some reason – otherwise nothing makes sense."

"One of life's imponderables."

"What is?"

"Does anything every make sense?" Rory smiled. He knew Hannah was holding back but was prepared to wait. It was the long game.

The day after publication Hannah received a card depicting the Madonna and child through the post. Inside was written: *Thank you so much, Mia x*

James also rang her. "Didn't realise that rag actually had a soul. Thank you Hannah."

"What for?"

"For treating the subject so sensitively and being so respectful of Mia. Anyway must go that's my bleep. See you soon."

I hope so, Hannah thought. She hadn't seen James since he'd brought Mia to see her. What was the real relationship between the cousins? She tortured herself with the obvious possibility. It had never occurred to her that James may have been or was still involved with someone else. What an idiot she was for thinking he was there waiting for her to beckon him to do her bidding. And Mia seemed such a lovely woman.

THIRTY-SEVEN

"Hannah, good morning. I've been doing some digging about this charity your friend Liz was working for. Thought it might have some bearing on Patrick and I think it would be a good idea to get together and run through it."

Strangely this was the second call of the day that Hannah had received about WelcAf. The first had been from Rory and he'd biked over a whole ream of cuttings some from quite obscure – to her at least – publications. "Bike will be quicker that faxing this lot," Rory had said.

It never ceased to amaze Hannah how much money the journalists had at their disposal for couriers and cash incentives. "Remember, this story is ours Hannah," he meant *The News* – "I think we may be on to something. Catch up soon."

"Would you mind coming here?" Hannah asked Simon. "It makes it easier with the childcare."

"Of course. What time suits you?"

"Shall we say four this afternoon?" That way Hannah would have a cut-off point at six when Janet left. She knew Janet had a date that evening and would want to leave on time.

"Perfect. I have your address. See you then."

Hannah opened the envelope containing the cuttings. Whoever had done this trawl had been efficient indeed. Hannah started at the top and worked down in date order.

An hour later Hannah was begining to see a pattern emerging. None of the cuttings was totally condemnantory of the WelcAf outposts in Somalia. No publication made outright accusations but there were undercurrents of criticism. Read in isolation you'd probably think nothing was amiss. However reading them en masse like this, Hannah saw a body of complaints – and they all implied that some of the charity employees, if not actively involved in trafficking young girls, were at least complicit in what was going on. They were turning a blind eye to young girls going missing.

Hannah was appalled. No wonder Liz came home if she had these suspicions. But why hadn't she shared this with her. Unless she was protecting her. It was beginning to seem increasingly possible that she was murdered to silence her.

And Patrick would have been dead too, but for the intervention of one of the homeless people from the Bull Ring. Who had that been? Sherlock and his strange behaviour towards her came to mind. It was as though he had seen through her disguise but she wondered now if he was warning her off for her own good. He didn't blow her cover for whatever reason of his own. There was also a suggestion that he knew far more than he was letting on. He had mentioned someone asking questions and nosing around the day before Liz died.

The phone rang and Hannah picked up the handset distractedly.

"Hannah?"

"Yes, sorry."

"Simon Ryan." There was a pause before Hannah registered her caller.

"Oh hello Simon. Sorry I was miles away. What can I do for you? I thought you were coming here this afternoon."

"Well, I was but I'm now at St Thomas's. Patrick is conscious and would like to see you. The police are here obviously but he's made it clear he won't say anything before he's spoken to you."

"I see. I'll need to make some arrangements for my daughter and then I'll join you. How is he?"

"Not good. I'm not even sure he can remember anything or knows where he is but the doctors assure me it's okay for you to visit. The police – well DI Turner to be exact – aren't too pleased as you can imagine. And I don't suppose it will be long before the archdeacon knows what's going on."

"I'll be as quick as I can."

Hannah phoned Nicky to see if she could have Elizabeth. Fortunately the bad weather had kept her indoors as well as Janet. Hannah explained that Janet should take Elizabeth to Nicky's if she hadn't heard from her by 5.30 then she booked a cab and was on her way to St Thomas's hospital.

There was a commotion outside Patrick Ryan's private room. DI Turner was shouting into her phone while the nasty sergeant she'd met before was having a battle of wills with the archdeacon who had arrived before her and was demanding to see the priest. The constable on duty outside the room was the only one who seemed totally calm.

Hannah bypassed the others, showed the officer her passport as ID and went into the room. Not knowing what to expect she was taken aback by the scene which confronted her. Father Patrick looked as deathly white as she sheet which covered him. He appeared gaunt and confused. His brother, the picture of health, sat beside him holding a clipboard which had some scribbling on it.

A doctor introduced himself. "Don't look so worried – all this looks worse than it is. After all that time on a ventilator and having a tube down his throat, Patrick is finding very difficult to talk. He is trying to write but that is difficult for him too at the moment. Speech and coordination will improve day by day."

Hannah walked over to the bed and sat in the chair opposite Simon. She touched his hand. "Hello Patrick. Welcome back."

Patrick made an unintelligible sound as he stared into Hannah's face then turned and jerked his brother's arm. Simon moved the clipboard in front of Patrick and guided a pen into his hand. All Hannah could see was a page of scribbles. The only word she could just make out with difficulty was her own name that Patrick kept jabbing at with the pen. The fear in his eyes seared into her. She could feel it, taste it, almost touch it. Fanciful as it seemed.

She leaned towards him. "Patrick, do you know why Liz was killed?"

He nodded. "Tra… traf… traff-ick-ing." Hannah wasn't sure that that was what he had actually said or what she had assumed he would say. He looked as though he had totally exhausted himself by uttering just one word.

Hannah looked across the bed to Simon. He inclined his head slightly.

"It's okay Patrick you're safe now," he said as though to a young child.

The doctor came over and checked the montors still attached to his patient. He smiled down at Patrick. "You're doing really well, old chap. Your voice will get stronger very soon. But you need to get some rest now."

Hannah took this as her cue and stood up. "Goodbye Patrick. I'll come and see you tomorrow."

Simon also stood and walked her to the door. "There's no way I'm letting the archdeacon or DI Turner in here today. I won't have Patrick distressed; it could set him back." He lowered his voice, "We'll have to have that talk another time. I don't want to frighten you but please be on your guard in every sense."

Hannah could feel a cloak of fear descend upon her. "Do you think it will be okay to come back tomorrow?"

"Yes, please do. I'll phone you in the morning."

As she closed the door behind her she was aware of three faces turned towards her. "Well?" said Claudia Turner.

"He needs to sleep."

"I'd have thought he'd done enough of that for now," sneered the sergeant earning him a glare from his DI.

The archdeacon stared at her. "I thought I'd made it perfectly clear that this was none of your business, Ms Weybridge. The diocese…"

"The diocese can wait their turn." Hannah matched his stare. "He needs to speak to the police first." She turned to Claudia. "I think Patrick might need a bit more protection, Inspector."

The DI nodded to her sergeant. "Stay here until I organise some more cover." She turned to the archdeacon. "I suggest you go back to doing whatever it is you do and we'll call you once Reverend Ryan has agreed to see you."

Hannah admired her stance but could see that the Venerable Andrew Fawshore was not impressed. He looked furious. "I shall have words with the Chief Inspector," he said. Mustering all his dignity, he strode down the corridor.

"May I offer you a lift home, Hannah?"

Remembering Simon Ryan's warning, Hannah felt her usual resistance dissipate. "I'd love one, thank you."

They left the hospital together and made for the car park. Hannah was surprised that Claudia got into the driver's seat and opened the front passenger door for her.

"Lost your driver?" Hannah settled herself and fastened the seat belt.

"Like to keep my hand in." Claudia smiled. "You look shattered."

"Thanks."

"You know what I mean. I gather Patrick Ryan wasn't up to much?"

"No his voice was very weak and his handwriting on the clipboard they'd given him was all over the place. Virtually illegible apart from my name. Which is presumably why his brother rang me."

"I wonder if he has anything relevant to say."

"Well at least we'll know that soon. As a matter of interest, do you know who rescued Patrick and got him to the hospital."

"No I don't." This was said rather too quickly. Hannah glanced at the inspector and wondered how much she really knew.

"Well he saved Patrick's life, that's for sure."

They had hit the traffic on the Walworth Road and the car was crawling along. "I'm going to take the next left and get us out of this." Claudia indicated and they were soon going through a warren of back streets.

Hannah yawned then remembered her instruction to Janet. "Excuse me, I have to make a call," she said as she dialled her home number. Janet answered and Hannah told her to stay there as she would be home soon. "Could you phone Nicky and let her know?"

"Who's Nicky?"

"A friend I made when I was pregnant. She's been great at stepping into the breech when I need a babysitter."

"Must be hard, bringing up a child on your own. Don't think I could do it."

"It's easier when you earn enough to pay for childcare. And I wouldn't be without her."

Claudia smiled as she looked into the rearview mirror then scowled and took a sharp right turning. "Hang on to your seat," she commanded as she picked up the radiophone and barked a registration number at someone at the other end.

Hannah stared at her.

"We're being tailed. Sorry I should have picked up on it earlier."

The rest of the journey was a blur to Hannah. All she wanted to do was get home and hug her child. But was it even safe to return? To lead whomever it was to her home and child? She could hear the DI on the radio. Then suddenly she relaxed back into her seat and slowed down. She turned to Hannah and smiled. "Just had a police car intercept them. Hope their tyres are up to scratch."

Hannah realised her breathing had been so shallow she was in danger of passing out and took a long inhalation. "I don't understand…?"

"Maybe you – or I – perhaps both of us have been asking too many pertinent questions. Let's leave it for now. We've both had a stressful day. But we do need to talk properly Hannah."

THIRTY-EIGHT

"Hello Hannah. Tom. Something's come up and I need to speak to you. Phone me when you can and I'll ring you back. By the way, I don't suppose you've had your house cleaned recently so am sending a pro."

Hannah played the message over several times. Tom was obviously being ultra careful. Maybe too careful but she felt the hairs on the back of her neck tingle. She looked at her watch to judge when the best time to ring would be given the time difference. After seeing Patrick and then being followed, she was more on edge than ever. The doorbell rang.

She ran downstairs and looked through the spyhole before opening the door. The man standing there put a finger to his lips and smiled.

Hannah nodded and stood aside for him to enter. She waited in the hall until he came out of the sitting room and gave her the thumbs up sign. She walked into the room and sat on the settee, remembering the last time she had seen Graham Stradan. She had nearly fainted in terror as Tom had grabbed her and clamped his hand over her mouth before gently explaining that Graham was a friend, "special effects man" he had called him. That time Graham had found two bugs placed in her phones. Surely it hadn't happened again? She was so careful now. New locks, security grills, virtually no one allowed into the house.

It seemed an age before Graham returned to the sitting room. "Sorry Hannah, you've been bugged again. Not such a professional job this time. This one was under your phone in the sitting room and this one behind a picture in the hall. Everywhere else is clean."

Hannah shook her head in disbelief. "How?" The question hung between them stretching out into silence.

"My guess, and it is only a guess, is that they were placed in haste. Maybe someone who visited you..? Last time they were in your phones which takes a certain expertise... Depending on where you take phone calls or talk to people these ones wouldn't have revealed very much, would they?"

"I don't know... Anyway I hope they've been bored rigid with listening to Janet playing with Elizabeth in here." She managed a smile but she felt sick. Violated. It didn't make any sense. Or did it? "Would you be able to lift prints from them?"

"Possibly if it was an amateur job the perpetrator may have been careless. Want me to try?"

"Yes please."

Graham refused her offer of coffee. "How did Tom sound when you spoke to him?"

"I didn't."

"Didn't what?"

"Speak to him. Claudia Turner asked me." And he left before Hannah had the chance to question him further.

"Hannah you must be careful. Your name has come up on a list that…"

"What do you mean 'come up on a list'? What sort of list and why the hell has it got anything to do with me?" Hannah could hear the screechiness in her voice and took a deep breath. "I'm sorry Tom. You've caught me at a bad time and I haven't a clue about what you are referring to."

Tom had rung her from a safe phone. He hadn't been able to get hold of Graham so had passed on his request through Claudia. Fortunately she didn't ask why but maybe she had ideas of her own. She had passed on the all clear message.

"Something I've been working on here threw up the name of the charity Liz was working for and your name was linked to it. You could be in danger, Hannah. I can't tell you any details but none of it is good. What have you been meddling in?"

"I haven't been 'meddling' as you call it in anything." She pronounced each word with an icy clarity. "I have been doing my work as a journalist. I wrote a piece about the charity when Liz was murdered."

"And?" Tom sounded tired and irritated.

"And nothing."

"Yes there is. You wrote an article recently on FGM – remember?"

"How do you know about that?"

"We get all the UK newspapers here."

"Well, that was nothing to do with the charity."

"Are you sure? Hannah I know you, you're making links. This is a can of vipers you've opened. I just wish…" She never heard what he wished for as the line went dead.

Hannah stood there, holding the receiver. She put it back in the cradle, thought for a moment than picked it up again. Her line was dead. Someone had cut her line. She grabbed her mobile and checked on Elizabeth sleeping in her room.

Walking into her own bedroom without turning on the light she skirted the walls until she reached the window and looked out into the darkness illuminated in parts by the street lamps and lights from the houses opposite. A young couple was strolling down the street arms around each other. A dog-walker paused by a lampost. A car door opened and closed. Nothing out of the ordinary. Yet there was something she couldn't see but she could feel it. And it chilled her to the marrow.

The next morning the landline was working again. She phoned British Telecom to see what the problem had been but was assured there had been no break in the service. She had not imagined it.

She looked at the card Graham "Special Effects" Stradan had given her while Janet got Elizabeth ready for Tiny Tots Club.

"You look worried, Hannah. Anything I can help with?"

Hannah smiled. "No it's nothing just the phone was playing up yesterday." She thought for a moment. "I think we ought to get you a mobile, Janet. Just in case it happens again. I know I'm paranoid and overprotective but…"

"But better to be prepared for all eventualities, don't you think, Elizabeth?"

"No," came the resounding reply.

"Her favourite word at the moment." Janet laughed and ticked the toddler. "Come on then, let's hit the road."

Hannah gave her daughter a hug and as soon as the door was shut behind them, she phoned Graham using her mobile. Graham answered on the third ring. "Stradan."

"Hello Graham. Hannah Weybridge here. I think I may have a problem."

Graham had arrived within the hour. However before then Hannah had received another perplexing phone call.

"Hannah – Celia Rayman. I'd like you to come here as soon as you can. There's something I need to show you." It was quite unlike Celia to be so curt – to the point of rudeness. Hannah agreed to go as soon as possible.

She was still thinking about what Celia might have to show her when Graham arrived.

He handed her a mobile phone. "Just bought this – a pay-as-you-go. New and clean."

"Thanks Graham. I think Tom's call to me was intercepted yesterday evening. The line suddenly went dead. This morning it was working again and BT says there had been no problem."

Graham's face looked grim. "That would have to have come from a local exchange. I'll look into it, Hannah but for now be wary of anything you say on the landline. Don't stop using it or we'll alert whoever's doing this. But make any sensitive calls on your mobile. By the way," he said as he was doing up his coat, "I lifted some prints from the bugs but they didn't show up on any police records. Sorry."

Hannah ignored that statement. She had a more pressing concerns. "Tom said my name's come up on a list. Something to do with the charity Liz worked for. WelcAf. I just don't understand…"

"I think you need to talk to DI Turner, Hannah. Be straight with her about anything you've found. You can trust her."

But can I? Hannah thought after Graham had left and she booked a minicab to take her to Kensington.

THIRTY-NINE

Sam Lockwood made his way down the narrow staircase of WelcAf HQ in Hammersmith. He was no nearer discovering what had happened to the information Liz Rayman had brought back to the UK. It struck him that he may have been set up. Perhaps she brought nothing back with her? He couldn't for the life of him believe she had been murdered because of her work in Somalia but…

That journalist Hannah Weybridge had been cagey. There was something quite unpleasant about the way she had dismissed him. Maybe he should have confided in her. Sought her help. He kicked himself for his gaucheness. But he was a medic not a bloody snoop.

He thought about ringing her to ask if she would meet him again. Couldn't do any harm; she could only say no.

He took his mobile out of his pocket along with her card and began tapping in the number. The afternoon darkness made him pause underneath a street light. He pressed connect and stepped out into the road.

He never saw the car speed out from a side turning. He felt the impact of hard steel against his body then nothing more.

By the time the police and ambulance had appeared, there was a protective ring around the body, parts of which were at strange angles. Blood had trickled from his nose and the light rain had joined forces with it. The crowd was strangely quiet as they moved back to allow the professionals in. Someone felt for a pulse then shook his head. Police tape had already cordoned off the area. A uniformed officer was taking down the names and addresses of bystanders. Most were stunned into silence except one elderly woman was shouting the odds. She looked as though she'd had a few too many but there was no mistaking her message.

"That effing car aimed itself at that man. It picked up speed and never stopped. It's murder, I say." And she kept muttering "murder" under her breath as the officer led her to one side.

Photographs were being taken of the corpse. Another officer watched and as the flash lit up the body again he saw something in the dead man's hand. He put on a glove and gently removed the business card and placed it in an evidence bag. As he did so he noticed the name. Hannah Weybridge – a bell rang in his memory. Was she the woman who had been involved with…

Just as he was making the connections he realised that someone was sobbing loudly right by the tape. He turned and saw a young woman wearing a huge woollen wrap and Doc Martens, with rings on all the fingers he could see clutching at a screwed up tissue and a man in a smart light grey suit. Neither was dressed for the weather and must have come out of one of the buildings.

As he approached them, the man, ashen faced, spoke. "He was one of our field workers. Sam Lockwood."

"And you are, sir?"

"Michael Dresdon, CEO of WelcAf Charity. Our offices are just behind us. Sam had just been to visit us prior to his return to Somalia." He handed the officer a card. "My contact details."

"Thank you sir. Do you know who his next of kin is?"

"Well he's not married so I suppose that must be his father. All his details will be on record in our office."

"Perhaps you could wait for the investigating officer, there? It would save a lot of time."

"Of course." He put his arm around Cheryl and led her back to the anonymous door through which they disappeared.

The officer stared after them. Coincidence? The murdered dentist Liz Rayman had worked for this charity. Her friend Hannah Weybridge had written about her death in *The News*. And now Sam Lockwood is mown down by a hit and run driver with her business card in his hand. He turned as he saw a plain clothes officer walking towards him. Maybe this info would help his promotion prospects.

"Okay constable …

"Fielding, Guv."

The CID officer smiled. "So Constable Fielding what have you got for me?"

Fielding opened his notebook and began reiterating the facts as he knew them… He handed over Michael Dresdon's business card and the evidence bag holding Hannah Weybridge's.

"Good work." The officer made some notes in his own book including the constable's number. "Right I'll go and see what Mr Dresdon has to say."

FORTY

Mary Cuthrington answered the door and led Hannah into the drawing room where Lady Rayman was sitting, looking at a photograph of Liz. She stood up as Hannah entered. Mary closed the door but from the inside – she was evidently a party to whatever was going on.

"Hannah, thank you so much for coming. I didn't want to discuss this over the telephone." She kissed Hannah on the cheek and guided her to sit on the sofa with her.

"Just as well, Celia. I recently discovered that someone had planted some bugs in my house."

The two older women exchanged glances. "DI Turner sent someone here to check. There was a device in the room you were using, Hannah," Mary said.

Hannah wound a strand of hair around her finger. "I'm so sorry."

"You have no need to apologise, Hannah. Whatever our daughter was engaged in has exposed you to danger as well. I hope you can forgive us for involving you." Celia had been holding

Hannah's hand and now looked near to tears. So unlike her usual self. "What I am going to tell you is confidential. I – we – have complete faith in your discretion."

Confused, Hannah looked from Celia to Mary. Were they, as she had once thought, in a relationship? And why tell her now?

"Hannah you once asked me about Lord Rayman and whether I thought Liz was looking for her father among the homeless people she treated."

"Yes, and you told me that Liz knew exactly what had happened. End of story."

Celia looked across at Mary who was sitting opposite them. She was smiling at Hannah.

"Mary..?" Celia prompted. Mary still said nothing. "My husband didn't desert me, Hannah. He went away for a while and returned as Mary Cuthrington, my companion."

"I don't understand... I..." Hannah was at a loss as to how to respond and wasn't even sure she understood what she was being told. Was Mary a transexual?

As if reading her thoughts Mary said, "I'm transgender, Hannah." She let that fact sink in before adding, "I always knew I had been born into the wrong body. For as long as I can remember. But I tried to live my life as a man. I married Celia and we were blessed with a daughter. But I couldn't carry on living a lie..."

"So we agreed that Lord Rayman should disappear. Mary had the treatment and operations and eventually returned to us. For which I am truly grateful." She smiled across at Mary.

"Liz always said it was like she had two mothers..." she mused.

"We told Liz as soon as she was old enough to understand and it has been our secret ever since." Mary went over and sat at the other side of Hannah. "I hope this hasn't upset you, dear?"

"No, not at all. But why tell me now? There was no need."

Celia stood and walked across the room to where some envelopes were piled on a side table. "I found these this morning. Almost by chance. They were tucked in a box file with miscellaneous papers. In one envelope addressed to us there was another, addressed to you. Our letter was mostly personal but did touch on what Liz had uncovered in Somalia. She asked us to pass on your letter personally. As we have no idea what it might contain, we decided to be honest about us. In the hope that you would respect our confidence."

"That goes without saying Celia, Mary."

"Well, I don't know about you Mary but I could do with a drink. Shall we go and organise some while Hannah reads her letter?"

Hannah was unprepared for the papers in the envelope. There was just a short personal message from Liz entreating her to take any action she could as a journalist to expose the trafficking of young girls – children – as sex slaves. The enclosed papers detailed the routes used by the perpetrators. It seemed that after the girls had been raped and abused by the terrorists, they were sold on to syndicates who transported them across the world, many of them to the UK, Europe and the US. Hannah found a timeline detailing the routes – and a list of names and addresses where some of the girls had ended up.

Hannah was unaware that Mary and Celia had returned until a handkerchief gently dabbed the tears from her face and a glass of brandy was held to her lips.

"Don't say anything dear," Mary said, "but please honour anything our daughter has asked of you."

Hannah nodded. "I need to get to an office. I'll go to *The News*. I can make copies of this and have them couriered to safe places. I won't take this home. And I'll need to speak to the police."

Her mobile rang. As if on cue it was DI Turner. "Hannah I need to speak with you."

When Hannah explained where she was and that she was heading for the newspaper offices, Claudia said she would collect her and take her there. They could talk en route.

DI Turner was taken aback by Hannah's appearance. She looked terrified. She wondered if she'd already heard the news about Sam Lockwood.

"Hannah I'm sorry to have to tell you this but Sam Lockwood was killed by a hit and run driver earlier today."

Hannah said nothing, just stared. "It was outside the offices of WelcAf and he had just called your number on his mobile. Did you speak to him?"

"So it's beginning …"

"What's beginning, Hannah?"

"The cull."

"The cull? What on earth do you mean?"

Hannah sniffed and wiped her tears with the back of her hand. "Claudia. I can't tell you at the moment. There's something I must do first and then, I promise you, you'll know everything."

"Are you aware I could have you in for questioning, for withholding evidence?"

"Why would you want to do that?" Hannah looked perplexed. "You'll have everything in a couple of hours. Just give me that. Please Claudia."

Hannah had phoned ahead and Rory had a vacant office ready for her. "Right what can I do to help?"

"I need to make some photocopies and have them couriered to certain people."

"No problem." He walked her to the photocopying machine.

"I know this sounds daft, but would you mind standing here with me until it's done."

Rory had not commented on Hannah's distraught appearance. He knew now he'd been right about that thread of steel which ran through her. Hannah collected the copies and followed Rory to the office. Hannah had made six copies, three of which she placed in envelopes, within envelopes writing a brief note to the recipient not to open unless instructed to – or if anything happened to her. The three other copies she put into her bag. One was for DI Turner. The other for Simon Ryan. He, if anyone, would know what to do with the information.

Rory had booked the couriers who had arrived at reception. Hannah went with Rory to despatch her envelopes. She wasn't leaving anything to chance. Each envelope had to be signed for by the recipient. Hannah then returned to the office, logged on to the computer and began writing.

Two hours later she was more or less satisfied with her work and printed it out. Three times. She gave one copy sealed in an envelope to Rory, asking him not to read it – yet. "It will probably be spiked anyway," she said in an attempt at humour. One copy she would give to Simon Ryan in person. The other she'd keep.

"Right, I need to get to St Thomas's Hospital now. I promised I'd visit Patrick Ryan."

"Do you think you're up to it Hannah? You look exhausted."

She smiled sadly. "It'll all soon be over."

"Okay I'll get you a car.

"Thanks Rory. For your support – everything." Hannah looked as though she was about to burst into tears. Instead she stood on tiptoes and kissed him on the cheek.

The car got her to St Thomas's in record time. She took the lift to Patrick's floor then stopped short. Outside his room was a large group of people, some in hospital uniform, some police and there was Simon Ryan looking the picture of fury.

"My brother is dead due to your ineptitude. How dare you say..."

What he was about to reveal was lost as everyone turned to the sound of Hannah collapsing in a spectacular faint.

She came round to find herself sitting on a chair with a nurse either side.

Simon Ryan knelt in front of her. "I'm sorry Hannah – I never intended for you to hear like that." He held her hand. "We need to talk but not now. I have to stay here for a while. You go home and I'll call you." His face bore the signs of grief as well as rage.

"But how? How did he die? I thought he was getting better."

"He was. Look, I'll call you as soon as I can. But please be on your guard."

"Take this." Hannah handed him the envelope. "Please keep it safe."

A nurse, having made sure she was ok standing, escorted her out of the building.

"I'm sorry for the loss of your friend. Will you be okay getting home?" she asked.

"Yes, I'll get a cab. Thank you."

FORTY-ONE

"Do I look like someone who cares?"

A sniff followed a hiccough. "No I suppose not. But I thought…"

"Just what did you 'think', Judy? I've noticed how petty and nasty you've been towards Hannah."

"But…" Judy didn't finish her justification when she saw the editor's raised eyebrow.

"You may not like it, Judy, but Hannah brings in a fresh perspective. She may not always get it right but she writes from the heart which is something you'd do well to emulate."

Judy opened and closed her mouth.

"For God's sake get a grip. Okay so you've made a fool of yourself with some man. It's not the first time…"

"But it's more than that. Honestly George–" she only just remembered to stretch the name – "ina, I didn't know he'd been involved with Hannah. And I certainly didn't know that he was being manipulated by some sort of syndicate he owed money to." Judy blew her nose. "This is serious. I'm shit scared."

"For whom? Yourself?"

"Yes of course but for Paul and Hannah too. And the child." Judy paused. "These are seriously nasty people. They'll stop at nothing to get what they want."

"And what do they want, in your considered opinion?"

The irony wasn't lost on Judy but she hadn't thought George would be such a cow towards her. They had worked together a long time. That had to count for something.

"I believe they think Hannah has in her possession information about the trafficking of young girls from the Somalian base where Liz Rayman was working. Apparently Liz worked out what was happening and documented the evidence. These people are convinced she passed this information on or at least brought it back with her from Somalia with the intention of exposing the perpetrators."

"Hence her murder?"

Judy nodded. She was feeling sicker by the moment.

"And you believe Hannah herself is at risk?"

"I know she is. But I'm not sure how much she knows or even if she has a clue about what is happening."

"I see." The editor pressed a number on her phone and barked a command to her secretary. The legal team and senior editoral staff would be joining them within minutes.

"You don't give Hannah credit for much, do you Judy? Judging by her past experiences and what Rory has hinted at, she is far more aware than you think. But that, sadly probably makes her far more vulnerable. Time to call in the big boys."

Judy had no idea to what she was referring but took this as her dismissal and stood up.

"No stay where you are. You can support your claims and then I will have you escorted to a safe place. No phone calls. Nothing – do I make myself clear? Hand over you mobile."

Judy looked about to protest then thought better of it. She rummaged in her bag and placed the mobile on the desk. She looked about to burst into tears again.

"Oh for heaven's sake stop grizzling woman. At least you may have saved your job by coming to see me now."

Judy swallowed the bile which rose in her throat. Paul bloody Montague had a lot to answer for.

Paul Montague banged on the door. His face bore a look of grim determination. As soon as Janet opened the door slightly he pushed his way in almost knocking her over in the process.

"Where's Hannah?"

Janet folded her arms and stood blocking the stairs. "She's not here at the moment but she'll be back soon. Please leave. You can wait in your car."

"I'm not waiting anywhere. Where's Elizabeth?"

Janet stood her ground. "She's sleeping."

"Get her." Janet didn't move but her face betrayed her fear. "Now!"

Paul stared at her. "I haven't got time for this." He pushed Janet aside and raced up the stairs. Janet could hear him going into Elizabeth's room and the murmur of his voice. Then he was back cradling Elizabeth in his arms awkwardly. "Where's her car seat?"

Janet had moved to the front door barring his exit. "For God's sake woman get out of my way." He placed Elizabeth on the floor and yanked Janet aside. She kicked him in the shins but to no avail. He had the door open and he had Elizabeth.

Janet could feel her blood draining from her. Whatever she did might hurt Elizabeth. The child was suspiciously quiet and looked at her with startled eyes. Suddenly she wailed. The sound galvanised her into action but Paul was too quick for her. "Mama" was the last word she heard.

The phone range three times, as arranged. One minute pause and then the phone was answered on the first ring.

"Target not at location."

"Abort mission."

"Too late."

The man in the grey suit. Dialled another number. "Where the fuck is target? Find and eliminate."

FORTY-TWO

Hannah gazed out of the taxi window. Unfamiliar streets passed by – too fast for her to catch the place names.

"Excuse me," she tapped on the glass dividing the driver from his pasengers.

He slide back the glass and at the same time she heard the click of the door locks and saw the red light indicating them.

"Yes miss?"

"I was just wondering which route you are taking. We seem to be taking a long time..."

"Just following instructions. Won't be long now."

"Instructons? Whose intructions? I don't understand." An icy grip of fear enveloped her body as the driver closed the connecting window with a resounding thud. Do they lock them, she wondered? She pulled out her mobile phone. No signal. Just what she needed. She stared at the license plate committing the number to memory. 74829. Don't panic, she told herself but already the early evening darkness was complete and she had absolutely no idea where she was or where she was heading. She tried to breathe deeply to exhale her fear so she could think what to do.

She'd hailed the taxi in front of the hospital so how could the driver be "following instructions"? It didn't make sense.

Who knew she'd be there at that precise time? Only someone who was watching her movements. She felt the bile rise in her throat.

She leaned forward and hammered on the glass partition. The driver didn't even look round but she saw him glance up at the rear view mirror. His eyes revealed nothing. He was safe in his driver's seat and she was trapped.

The red locked lights glared at her. Don't waste your energy she thought. Save it. Think.

But no solutions presented themselves. Her mind was full of terrible visions and thoughts of what might happen to her. She could feel her pulse racing and her arms felt weak from the rush of adreneline. Elizabeth. Oh God Elizabeth. Don't cry. Don't show any weakness. But she felt as feeble as a baby. Her hands were clammy, she tasted the acidic bile which filled her mouth and wanted to spit it out. Eventually she found some tissues and retched into them. It didn't bring any relief.

Her whole body was frozen in time and space but she could feel a trickle of sweat make its way from her armpits. Her sweat must give out the scent of her distress. Hormones. There was nothing she could do except wait to see where they arrived. No that would be too late. She thought of Elizabeth. She had to be proactive not accept her fate whatever it was.

She moved as though to stand up, making sure the driver looked at her then collapsed onto the floor of the cab and flayed around. Her body jerked and spittle escaped from her mouth.

The taxi pulled up abruptly and she slid across the floor. The driver opened the door. She was ready for him. "Fucking hell."

With a strength that she dredged up from the core of her being, Hannah lurched towards him and aimed a kick at his crotch, catching him completely off guard. "You bitch," he yelled as she swiped him round the head with her bag and every ounce of energy she could muster. He reeled backwards onto the pavement, curling up into a ball. She gave him another kick for good measure and then ran back in the direction they had come from hoping with every particle of her being that he wouldn't follow her.

The blood pounded in her ears. She could hardly breathe. Her lungs were burning but her legs kept moving. Finally she came to a corner and checked the street name. She was in Concord Close. She scrabbled in her bag for her mobile phone. She had some signal… Three nines.

"Which service do you require caller?"

"Police…" There was a short pause.

"Hello caller where are you?

"Concord Close E15. My name is Hannah Weybridge and I need to get a message to DI Turner. I was abducted by a man driving a taxi cab … he…"

"Hold on Ms Weybridge… There's a police car in your vicinity. Stay where you are. They'll pick you up within two minutes."

Hannah leaned back against the wall and sobbed in relief. She heard the distant wail of a siren which grew louder. The car went straight past her but had slowed down enough to catch her frantic wave and reversed.

"Hannah Weybridge?"

She nodded before her legs buckled and she fell into the arms of the officer. "You're OK now." He guided her towards the car and lowered her into the back seat. "Put your head between your knees and take slow breaths."

She did as she was told and gradually her head stopped swimming.

"Do you need medical attention?" She shook her head. "Right we'll get you home then."

"The license number. The taxi driver's license number was 74829."

The officer smiled. "Blimey well done." He relayed the information over the radio along with the name of the road the taxi had been travelling down.

Meanwhile the driver put the car into gear and did a u-turn. "Okay let's get you back to East Dulwich."

"How do you know where to take me?"

"There was an alert put out for you, Miss."

"Really?" Waves of relief cascaded over her. She closed her eyes. "DI Turner?"

"She's gone straight to your address."

"Thank God," Hannah breathed deeply and remembered nothing more of the journey home.

The police car pulled up at the corner of her street which was cordoned off with police tape. As she got out she was aware of people huddled together. An gaseous stench filled the air. Somewhere a dog barked. Beyond the tape Hannah could make out a fire engine and an ambulance. They both seemed to be parked outside her house.

Her pulse pounded so hard in her ears she could hear nothing else. Her legs refused to move. Then she could hear screaming. A high pitched wail that went on and on. Would it never stop?

The slap across her face echoed in the street. "Hannah it's okay. Hannah listen to me."

The cordon was lifted and she was led, half carried by Claudia Turner.

Coming towards her was Paul Montague, one arm around Janet, the other holding her child. Elizabeth. Their child. She felt her knees give way as a paramedic leaped forward to guide her to a chair and handed her a cup of water.

"Hannah I'm so sorry, I…" Paul had no chance to continue.

"Give me my child. Now."

Paul placed Elizabeth into her arms as Hannah wept. "I'm so so sorry my darling," she whispered. Miraculously, Elizabeth just smiled up at her. Hannah was conscious that Janet was hovering nearby. She looked like an extra from a horror film. Her hair was all over the place. Dirt on her face. A long rip in her jeans.

"Janet are you okay? What on earth happened?"

"Hannah I tried to stop him – I really did – but he saved our lives." She looked terrified. "We're both okay just a couple of bumps and bruises."

"I'm so sorry, Janet. I…"

A police officer interrupted her. "We'll take you home now Miss and you can make your statement."

Janet leaned forward and hugged Hannah and Elizabeth. "I've got the mobile," she whispered. "Call me on that."

Hannah wondered how the phone had managed to escape damage but just nodded. There was too much to take in. As Janet was led away, she realised that Paul was being read his rights and was wearing handcuffs.

"Paul?"

He turned to her and shrugged. "I'm sorry Hannah. I really am."

DI Turner was beside her. "Claudia what is going on?"

"Long story, Hannah. And I think you know most of it. Except Paul's part in all this."

"But what has he done? Janet just said he got them out of the house – just in time."

"We'll know more once he's been interviewed, Hannah, but believe me he's mixed up in this mess."

Hannah was aware of movement around her. The position of the cordon had been moved and some people were returning to their homes. Even the houses either side of hers were now okay.

The chief fire officer approached them. "It was a small explosion Inspector. Some minor damage. I'll get a full report to you asap."

Claudia nodded and turned to Hannah. "Right. Let's get you somewhere safe for the night." She took a call on her radio phone. "Yes sir," she concluded.

"Your fairy godfather has contacted the Commissioner. No expense spared for your temporary accommodation." Hannah didn't understand. She clutched Elizabeth to her. The child was alseep as though nothing untoward had happened.

"I'll be informed of the venue within about twenty minutes. Why don't we sit in my car, then we'll be ready to go."

"Can I collect some things from my home?"

"No but don't worry we've been instructed to get you anything you need."

Once they were ensconced in the car, Hannah tried to make some sense of what had happened. "Claudia I don't understand. What happened?"

Claudia studied her for a moment as if judging how much to reveal. "It seems a letter bomb of some description was delivered to you home. In a jiffy bag. It would seem that Paul Montague found out about it and came over to warn you. Only just in time. It didn't detonate properly so the damage isn't too bad. Either someone wanted to scare the hell out of you or put an end to your enquiries."

Liz. Jacob Gurnstein. Sam Lockward. Patrick. All dead. And she would have been too.

Hannah leaned forward to fish out the papers from her handbag. "This is what I said I would let you have, Claudia." Claudia glanced at the envelope and put is safely in her brief case.

"It's the informaton Liz amassed in Somalia. I've sent copies to some safe addresses plus I've also written an article for *The News* – although I don't suppose they'll publish it."

"We'll see," was all the DI said as she received a message on her radio and her driver put the car into gear and they were off.

FORTY-THREE

"Gas explosion! Gas explosion my arse! And we're supposed to go along with that?"

Rory was on his feet. His whole body rigid in outraged disbelief.

"Yes we are." Larry Jefferson from the legal department spoke with a quiet authority. "We don't want to put Hannah at any more risk."

"And where is she now?"

"Somewhere safe. The fewer people who know where, the better. For the time being at least." Georgina actually looked like she wanted to cry. A definite first.

"I take it we are covering the story?"

"Of course we are, Hannah is one of us." The editor looked around the room daring anyone to contradict her. "And this is a major news story. You'll write it Rory. Based on the official version of events of course. Then we'll add references to what has been going on – behind my back it would seem – to have the edge on the other papers. We'll have to be devious but it shouldn't be beyond our combined capabilities. Our copy will be checked by the appropriate authorities. Lot of good they've been so far." Georgina looked down at her bitten nails. "Okay let's get going we've only got a short lead on the other papers... We won't go with the early edition to avoid spoilers."

There was a scraping of chairs. The deputy editor looked even more absent-minded professor than usual. "Where's Judy, by the way, or am I missing something?"

"She's on gardening leave..." Georgina said nothing more but snapped her fingers and pointed at the door. Larry Jefferson was the last to leave as another man entered the office by the opposite door. He was short in stature but exuded power and a confident authority.

"So what do we think?" Lord Gyles asked.

"I think we do everything we can to support Hannah. I have no idea what had happened to her last year after we spiked that exposé of hers but that was yet another cover up. God knows what she's going through now. We've still got that story. We could use it as leverage now."

"We could indeed. I'll make a few calls." He paused. "No I'll make a few visits."

"Better take some security with you."

"I always do." The proprieter smiled and stood up. "I take is we can trust everyone who was in this room?"

"What do you think?"

"I never assume, do you?"

She shook her head. "No, never."

He left by the door he'd come in by. Just before it clicked shut, it opened again. "Be careful George."

"You too." She put her head in her hands and breathed out slowly. There was a knock on the door and Rory entered looking flustered.

"Georgina – you need to read this."

"What is it?"

"It's an article Hannah wrote here this afternoon. She sent copies of the documents it's based on to various addresses. As insurance. She asked me not to read it – but under the circumstances…"

"Thanks Rory." She scanned the pages. "We won't be able to print any of this yet but you can allude to parts of it in your copy."

She smiled. "What a resourceful woman. Lord Gyles will be glad she's on our team."

FORTY-FOUR

Hannah woke up and for a moment it seemed that the horror of the night before had not happened. Elizabeth was curled up beside her in the king size bed. The hotel had provided a cot in the room but Hannah wanted her child close to her. She looked at her now, sleeping peacefully. The thought of what might have been was too awful to contemplate.

From the sparse facts Claudia had given her, it seemed she was the target. And when it was realised she wasn't at home, whoever was behind all this had arranged for the taxi to collect her at St Thomas's. The memory of that nightmare journey sent shock waves through her. Claudia had been amazed at her escape plan and that it had succeeded.

The police had found and arrested the taxi driver soon after she had been picked up. Apparently he hadn't known much but had been generously paid for his service.

And Paul? How could he have been part of all this? How involved was he? Hannah's information had been that some of the trafficked girls from Somalia ended up as sex slaves in Europe including the UK. No matter how much she despised Paul for the way he had acted towards her, she couldn't believe he would be part of such a despicable syndicate. For that's what it was, a syndicate that used and abused young girls.

Elizabeth stirred beside her. Hannah stroked her cheek.

There was a discreet knock on the door. Hannah moved carefully out of the bed, put on the hotel bathrobe and went to the door. The plain clothes woman police officer who had settled her into the suite the previous evening smiled at her.

"I hope you managed to get some sleep, Ms Weybridge. It's eight o'clock and I wondered if you would like to order some breakfast. DI Turner should be here at 9.30, I think."

"Have you been here all night?"

The woman smiled. "No, I've just come back. But you've had someone here all night."

Hannah walked through into the enormous sitting room complete with dining table and chairs. She didn't feel hungry but knew she'd have to eat and ordered from the breakfast menu with some extras for when Elizabeth woke up. "Are you having any…"

"Susan. No I've eaten but I join you with the coffee if that's ok and we can go through what you need delivered."

"How long do you think we'll be here?"

"I really don't know. We'll have a better idea when the DI arrives."

While she was waiting Hannah had a quick shower in one of the most luxurious bathrooms she'd ever seen. There was a walk-in shower, a huge bath, bidet and enough mirrors to saistfy the most committed narcissist. Plus there were toiletries and just about anything a guest would conceivably need. Last night she'd had a bath and her clothes had been taken away for laundering. They were in the bedroom waiting for her when she emerged.

"I could get used to this level of service," she said as she walked into the sitting room at the same time as the breakfast was delivered.

Susan murmered something to the waiter before he left.

"Do you know him?"

"One of us. We're taking no chances."

Hannah didn't know whether to feel reassured or even more frightened. Elizabeth's imperious call distracted her.

James walked over to the nurses' station and idly picked up a copy of *The News*. In a red box along the top of the front page he read: "Gas explosion in East Dulwich pages 2, 3 and 4".

He felt his stomach lurch and sat down quickly as he opened the paper. He scanned the story for Hannah's name which he found in the second paragraph. Only once he was assured there were no casualties did his breathing return to near normal. The article implied that the "gas explosion" – their quotes – was a cover and that journalist Hannah Weybridge, who was investigating the murder of her friend Liz Rayman, was a victim of a crime syndicate's retribution.

James looked up as a cup of tea was placed before him.

"You look as though you could do with more than this but it's all I have on offer." The ward sister picked up a file and left him alone.

The article also linked in the deaths of a tramp, Jacob Gurnstein, the priest Patrick Ryan and a medic who had worked in Somalia with Liz: Sam Lockward. It also mentioned that Paul Montague had been arrested and was helping the police with their enquiries.

Paul! What the hell was he doing in all this. James had quite liked him when he and Hannah were seeing each other. He'd noticed him at Liz's funeral but they hadn't spoken.

Without thinking, James picked up the phone and dialled Hannah's number. Then disconnected abruptly. The article stated she was currently in a safe house. He could only hope that was true. His thoughts turned to Mia. Was she safe? At least she hadn't been mentioned by name in the article Hannah had written. *God what a total mess.* And there was, it seemed, nothing he could do to help. He drank the tea which was now lukewarm and stood up. His whole body felt leaden with dread. But he still had a job to do.

Simon Ryan's grief for his brother was tempered by his need to do something. Anything. There was a rage boiling up in him which needed an outlet. After reading all the information Hannah had passed on to him, he had tried ringing Hannah but the number appeared to be disconnected. He tried her mobile but that just rang out.

He had phoned his mother last night which was just as well as he'd had a call from *The News* early this morning. They confirmed that Patrick's death had been linked to Liz Rayman's. Hannah was in a safe house somewhere after an explosion at her home. Apparently a colleague of Liz's had been killed by a hit and run driver.

What a nest of vipers, Hannah had exposed. To make it worse he personally knew two of the people on the list. Two men of high social standing, at the pinnacle of their careers. Two men who had allegedly bought young Somalian girls from some trafficking syndicate. If anything could make him change from defence to prosecution this would be it. Bastards. And his brother had been killed to keep their dirty secrets.

He thought back to the scene at the hospital. He'd walked into Patrick's room as a nurse was admistering an injection.

"What's that for?" he'd asked more for something to say than for the answer.

"A vitamin infusion," came the reply.

The male nurse had actually smiled at him. Then left the room. Two minutes later all hell broke loose as another nurse came in, started the obs then called the crash team, as she began pumping at Patrick's heart.

All to no avail. It looked as though Patrick had been murdered in front of his very eyes. His grief had given clarity to his anger. And then Hannah had arrived – and fainted.

His mobile ringing broke into his thoughts. DI Turner was calling to say she was on her way.

Well, the police had a lot to answer for. Not to mention hospital security.

He made several calls then sat down to wait.

FORTY-FIVE

Lady Celia Rayman had been contacted by the police. Hannah and Elizabeth were unharmed but there had been a minor gas explosion at their home.

"Apparently," she said to Mary after the call, "they are now in a safe house whatever that is."

Mary had tears running down her face. The two women clung to each other like reeds in a windswept lake. Neither of them spoke for a long time.

Then a courier arrived with an envelope. Inside was a copy of *The News* with a brief note from Lord Gyles. Side by side they sat and read the article together. Mary broke the unhappy silence between them.

"Poor Hannah. What she has been through - because of us."

Celia nodded. "But we couldn't have known, Mary. We couldn't have known. I wonder how much will actually come out. Our dear darling girl was so brave. I don't want her to have died in vain."

That evening on the early news a short item revealed that four young Somalian girls had been freed from a large, residential property in York. It was, the presenter commented, part of a wider and ongoing police investigation into trafficking. No other details were released.

At the end of the programme, a face both of them knew, appeared on the screen. The MP for Darlington South had resigned to spend more time with his family.

Celia and Mary looked at each other. Maybe Liz and Hannah would succeed after all.

Hannah had followed the news on the TV and in the newspapers. There was little she could do. After a mercifully brief interview with Claudia Turner, she was told it would be a couple of days before she could return home. It transpired that Lord Gyles, proprietor of *The News* was footing the bill for her hotel stay.

"I'd make the most of it, if I were you." Claudia smiled then her expression turned serious. "I wish you'd confided in me earlier, Hannah, but I understand why you didn't. Has Tom been in touch? I did leave a message for him?

"No I haven't heard from him since he … anyway I expect whatever he's working on is far too important." She sounded bitter and she knew it. But she didn't want Claudia's pity either. "Can I have my mobile back now?"

"Yes nearly forgot that." She delved in her bag and retrieved the phone. "By the way, the prints Graham lifted on the bugging devices found in your house…" Hannah nodded. "Matched with Paul Montague."

Hannah was silent. She'd already learned that Paul's involvement was to curry favour with Judy to find out what *The News* had on Liz's murder. She, it seems, was also his target. Nothing to do with wanting to see his daughter. Just acting to save his own neck. The bastard.

"We've been unable to trace the man Paul says instructed him. The address of the office he went to, was a room rented by the hour. We've been told to stand down now. MI5 have taken over. So I don't suppose we'll ever discover the whole story. But Hannah, you have liberated a number of girls whose lives have been almost destroyed. Some of them will be able to return home. All thanks to you."

Hannah's face gave only a ghost of a smile. "But not Liz or Patrick or Sam Lockwood."

That night the news featured an atrocity in Somalia. Trevor Macdonald announced: "An aid worker in an outpost in Somalia was brutally murdered. His mutilated body was found hanging from a tree in the local village. No one has been charged and no one is claiming responsibility. Although rumours suggest he may have had terrorist connections. We go over live to the offices of WelcAf the charity responsible for this NGO post."

Hannah watched Michael Dresdon in front of the WelcAf offices read out a prepared statement.

"Naturally I and my team are devasted by the news of Frank Stone's terrible death in Somalia. This is the third death of personel who worked at this station and for that reason we are evacuating all our staff there. While Liz Rayman and Sam Lockwood died in London we have been told that their murders are linked to events in Somalia. This is all I am able to say at this point in time. My thoughts and prayers are for the families and friends of our departed colleagues."

Hannah switched off the television. Presumably this Frank Stone was linked to the trafficking. She wondered who the perpetrators had been. Blaming terrorists was the easy option.

James had been to see her that evening. His usual bear hug was so welcome.

"How do you feel about being back home?" The implied question she thought was, is it safe?

"Relieved. Saddened. Worried… Half the time I don't know what to think. Claudia Turner wouldn't have let me return if she wasn't as sure as she could be of my safety. I notice the local bobbies walk down this street more often than before."

James chuckled. He looked more relaxed than she'd seen him for a while.

"And Tom thinks that MI5 have all bases covered. Whatever that means."

"You've heard from him then?"

Hannah was about to retort "obviously" but swallowed the word when she saw James's face. He looked stricken. "Yes I have. James, can I ask you something?"

"Ye-es. Don't guarantee answers…"

"Are you involved with Mia?"

"That's an odd question. Of course I am, she's my cousin."

"Nothing more?"

"She's my cousin, Hannah. And it's complicated."

"Sorry I didn't mean to pry. And thanks for calling in," she added as he stood to take his leave. "I do appreciate all you've done for me, James."

"Come here you idiot." He pulled her to him and kissed the top of her head. "Just aim for a quieter life. Please." He kissed her again and left for another long night shift at the hospital.

Sitting quietly in church, Hannah reflected on how much had changed since she'd last been there for Liz's funeral. Not to the church but to her life. And how close she'd come to losing everything. Although everyone kept assuring her she was safe now, she didn't quite believe it. All the precautions she'd taken after Gerry Lacon's attempt on her life she now redoubled. She didn't want to move house – anyone would still be able to find her if they had the resources. Deciding to stay put was an act of defiance. There in the church she almost prayed that she'd made the right decision.

Simon Ryan had asked her to meet him at the vicarge to discuss arrangements for his brother's funeral. He wasn't there when she arrived too early so she left a note and had walked round to St John's. Simon had been packing up Patrick's things and sorting his affairs. Apparently Patrick had left detailed instructions for his funeral. Seemed a bit morbid but perhaps that's what priests do. Another priest was saying evening prayers. Hannah had not joined the small group who sat with him but she returned the nods and smiles from Lucy, Beano and someone she vaguely recognised but didn't know the name of.

The service was soon over and she walked with Lucy and co out of the church. The afternoon was already dark. A flash almost blinded them. "Miss Weybridge? Anything to say about your friend's murderers?"

Hannah was blinded by another flash and could feel rather than see movement around her. Somebody positioned himself in front of her. The Cardboard City dwellers moved in closer. There was a scuffle. She heard someone fall heavily and a familiar voice shout, "Get after that photographer." A sound like a punch and a grunt.

"Okay let's add resisting arrest and assaulting a police officer to the list of charges."

The man in front of her was rock solid. He had not moved a muscle and she felt protected by his presence.

A siren sounded then the squeal of brakes. She still couldn't see a thing but she could sense the tension around her slowly dissipating. Someone was being led away.

Lucy clutched her hand. "You alright luv?" Hannah didn't trust her voice and nodded. "Where did you spring from Sherlock?" Lucy asked the man in front of Hannah.

"Just happened to be passing. Stroke of luck, don't you think?"

The church's exterior lights had been switched on and he turned and smiled at Hannah. Whoever he really was she didn't care. He… Hannah realised he was bleeding. He'd taken a bullet meant for her.

And then he was beside her. Tom. Tom who was never there when she needed him had turned up with only seconds to spare. He looked at Sherlock and called out for a paramedic to attend him. The other Cardboard City dwellers melted into the evening. Then she was in his arms. Sobbing. Slowly he guided her down the steps and into a car.

"So how did you know there was to be an attempt on my life?"

They were sitting side by side on the sofa. Tom leaned forward and poured some more wine in their glasses. "Some of this comes under the official secrets act. What I can tell you is that people we are investigating in the US are connected to your investigation into the child trafficking. Most of the perpetrators have been rounded up in the UK. But we got wind that someone in the US had been assigned to… to…" Tom took a large gulp of wine. "I was supposed to intercept him. But he gave me the slip at the airport."

Hannah sat silently absorbing these facts.

"I rang here and Janet told me you were meeting Simon Ryan at the vicarage. I went there first. I think the hitman had been waiting for you there then saw you go to the church. The guy with the camera was a distraction."

"But what about Sherlock? How did he know? I don't believe he had just been passing."

"He wasn't. He's an undercover officer. Working on something altogether different. Anyway his cover is probably blown now."

"Well he took that bullet for me. He must have been shot just as he moved in front of me and he never flinched. He must have the courage of a … of a … I can't think of a comparison."

"What a journo like you, lost for words?" Tom took her hand. "I'm so sorry I haven't been here for you, Hannah. Claudia did warn me but…"

"Claudia warned you! Oh for God's sake."

Tom looked at his watch. "My car will be here in five minutes."

"You're leaving?" Hannah couldn't believe her ears.

"I have to. But I should be back in six weeks or so."

"Don't rush on my account." Hannah stood up. She'd heard the car pull up outside.

They both walked into the hall. "Goodbye Tom. Take care."

His eyes bored into hers. The inches between them were the Atlantic Ocean.

"I'll be back." He kissed her fleetingly on the lips and was gone.

Hannah leaned back against the locked door then slid to the floor and sobbed until her tears subsided and she blew her nose loudly.

Wearily she climbed the stairs and slipped silently into Elizabeth's room. Her precious daughter didn't stir. But tomorrow – tomorrow they'd catch up on all the games and fun she'd missed out on recently. At least she had a tomorrow to look forward to.

ACKNOWLEDGEMENTS

First and foremost I must thank Matthew Smith of Urbane Publications. He agreed to publishing *Death's Silent Judgement* sight-unseen as a sequel to *Dancers in the Wind* which is an amazing compliment for an author. I finished writing the sequel just before publication of the first Hannah Weybridge thriller.

I owe a debt of immense gratitude to Sue O'Neill and Elisabeth Stevenson who read the manuscript. Sue, who had been one of my readers for *Dancers in the Wind*, checked for any inconsistencies with the first book and Elizabeth judged whether *Death's Silent Judgement* could be read as a stand-alone. They have both been fabulously supportive and encouraging during my darker moments.

In researching this book I am indebted to Ian Patrick who served in the Metropolitan Police in the 90s, Dr Geoff Lockwood, a consultant anaesthetist at the Hammersmith Hospital, who helped with medical questions and Revd Ben Rhodes for biblical references. Any inaccuracies are totally of my own making.

Thanks to friends who must have been bored rigid with my talking about writing Hannah's second story and to my daughter Olivia who, having read the first chapter, highlighted a problem. The remedy for this provided me with another sub plot...

And huge thanks to everyone who reads and buys books and to the amazing book bloggers and twitter friends who herald new books and introduce authors to a wider audience.

For most of her working life in publishing, Anne has had a foot in both camps as a writer and an editor, moving from book publishing to magazines and then freelancing in both.

Having edited both fiction and narrative non-fiction, Anne has also had short stories published in a variety of magazines including Bella and Candis and is the author of seven non-fiction books.

Born in Clapham, Anne returned to London after graduating and has remained there ever since. In an attempt to climb out of her comfort zone, Anne has twice "trod the boards" – as Prince Bourgrelas in Ubu Roi when a student and more recently as a nun in a local murder mystery production. She also sings periodically in a local church choir and is relieved when she begins and finishes at the same time – though not necessarily on the same note – as everyone else. Needless to say, Anne will not be giving up her day job as an editor and writer.

Telling stories is Anne's first love and nearly all her short fiction as well as Dancers in The Wind and Death's Silent Judgement began with a real event followed by a "what if ..." That is also the case with the two prize-winning 99Fiction.net stories: Codewords and Eternal Love.

Anne is currently working on the sequel to Death's Silent Judgement.